T0282255

Readers love
The Duke's Cowboy
by Andrew Grey

By ANDREW GREY

Accompanied by a Waltz
All for You
Between Loathing and Love
Borrowed Heart
Buck Me
Buried Passions
Catch of a Lifetime
Chasing the Dream
Crossing Divides
Dedicated to You
Dominant Chord
Dutch Treat
Eastern Cowboy
Hard Road Back
Half a Cowboy
Heartward
In Search of a Story
Lost and Found
New Tricks
Noble Intentions
North to the Future
One Good Deed
On Shaky Ground
Only the Brightest Stars
Paint By Number
Past His Defenses
The Playmaker
Pulling Strings
Rebound
Reunited
Running to You
Saving Faithless Creek
Second Go-Round
Shared Revelations
Survive and Conquer

Three Fates
To Have, Hold, and Let Go
Turning the Page
Twice Baked
Unfamiliar Waters
Whipped Cream

ART
Legal Artistry • Artistic Appeal
Artistic Pursuits • Legal Tender

BAD TO BE GOOD
Bad to Be Good • Bad to Be Merry
Bad to Be Noble • Bad to Be Worthy

BOTTLED UP
The Best Revenge • Bottled Up
Uncorked • An Unexpected Vintage

BRONCO'S BOYS
Inside Out • Upside Down
Backward • Round and Round
Over and Back • Above and Beyond

THE BULLRIDERS
A Wild Ride • A Daring Ride
A Courageous Ride

BY FIRE
Redemption by Fire
Strengthened by Fire
Burnished by Fire
Heat Under Fire

Published by DREAMSPINNER PRESS
www.dreamspinnerpress.com

Published by DREAMSPINNER PRESS
www.dreamspinnerpress.com

Published by DREAMSPINNER PRESS
www.dreamspinnerpress.com

The Viscount's Rancher

ANDREW GREY

DREAMSPINNER
PRESS

Published by
DREAMSPINNER PRESS

8219 Woodville Hwy #1245
Woodville, FL 32362 USA
www.dreamspinnerpress.com

The Viscount's Rancher
© 2024 Andrew Grey

Cover Art
© 2024 L.C. Chase
http://www.lcchase.com
Cover content is for illustrative purposes only and any person depicted on the cover is a model.

Trade Paperback ISBN: 978-1-64108-571-7
Digital ISBN: 978-1-64108-416-1
Trade Paperback published September 2024
v. 1.0

For Dominic, who sees me through all the challenges life throws our way.

CHAPTER 1

COLLIN STRODE across the late-regency-era stableyard to where his old school chum and friend, George, waited in the archway that led out to the rolling green of his estate. George was the master of all he surveyed, and Collin envied him. He wasn't *jealous*—no mean, backstabbing green-eyed monster—but he wished he was as *happy* as George.

"I love this view," George said just as his partner and soon-to-be husband burst out of the tree line and raced like the wind across the land, long hair bouncing with each stride of his horse. The envy strengthened as Alan continued his ride, back straight, head up and forward, like he was meant to control the beast he rode and anything or anyone who crossed his path.

"What's not to love?" Collin agreed, his gaze following Alan as he made a turn, the horse slowing as they approached. Alan's eyes were wide, his mouth split in a grin. He looked completely out of place surrounded by the other riders in English riding boots, leggings, and helmets. Alan wore jeans and chaps, a flannel shirt, and tooled cowboy boots that were unlike anyone else's in the area. The truth of it was that Alan was unlike anyone Collin had ever met. He was 100 percent his own man and he didn't give a damn what anyone thought, and that made him all the more attractive.

Of course, Collin would never give serious consideration to his fascination with the stunning cowboy. Collin didn't poach, and certainly not from a close friend.

Besides, Alan only had eyes for George.

Alan dismounted the black horse before bounding over and encircling George in his long arms, hugging him hard. It was a very un-English thing to do, and a very Alan spectacle that reminded Collin just how alone he was. The truth was, he wanted someone who would love him as much as Alan clearly adored George. There was no disguising that love, and Alan didn't try. The love the cowboy had for his duke was apparent to everyone who saw them together for more than ten seconds.

"The horse, how is he?" Collin asked, hoping his voice didn't break.

Alan backed away, still smiling as he handed the reins to Collin. "I have no idea what your father is thinking," he answered, his gaze suddenly all business. "He really wants to sell?"

Collin sighed and nodded. "He says he'll never work for polo, and that's what he wanted him for. Not that Jester here is actually his horse. He's mine, officially, but the stable is my father's, so...." Sometimes Collin wished his sire, the Earl of Doddington, would simply stop being a complete controlling wanker.

"He's a fool, and so are you if you sell him," Alan said. "This boy was born to run. It's in his blood, even if it's not in his bloodline. It's what he wants. So if you don't want to sell him, then we'll make a place for him here and we can put him into training as a racer with Centauri. He has the drive and the strength. You saw him; he went like the wind. And let me tell you, he didn't want to stop." Alan was dead serious.

"It *would* get under the old man's skin if I actually raced him and won." The thought delighted him.

Alan chuckled. "Don't get ahead of yourself, but I'd say he definitely has potential."

Glenn, one of the horse wranglers, approached and spoke with Alan briefly before leading Jester away.

"He'll take good care of him."

"Thank you," Collin said. "I knew you'd have some sort of answer. I didn't want to sell him. He was a gift from my uncle."

Alan nodded as though he knew the story. Collin's mother's brother, Uncle Reginald, had given him Jester as a colt two years ago. Reginald died of cancer two months later. Collin's father had hated Uncle Reginald with a passion, though Collin had no idea why, so it didn't take much thought to determine why his father wanted Jester gone. Alan usually tried to keep him out of Collin's father's sight.

"We understand," George said. "Come on. It's getting cold, and with this constant drizzle, I could use something hot." Alan bumped his hip. "To *drink*," George emphasized wickedly. "Come on. Let's go in." He led the way to the Rover, and Alan got behind the wheel. Collin braced himself, because every time George let Alan drive, Collin wondered if he was going to remember to use the left side of the road. Alan had a tendency to take his half out of the middle. It was fine on the estate, because everyone watched out for him, but on the roads....

"Don't worry. I've got driving on the wrong side the road down now," Alan quipped.

"Sure you do, big guy," Collin teased, and Alan turned to flash him a grin before starting the engine and driving sedately—on the correct side the road—all the way up to the great house. He parked the car, and they went in the private entrance and through to the family apartments, which were closed to the touring public.

"The estate is open today," Alan explained. "George will go down at some point to say hello." He closed the door, his boots clomping on the stone floor until he took them off. They climbed the familiar stairs to a comfortable sitting room in the south wing on the second floor.

"What can I get you?" Alan asked. "I can call down for coffee or tea."

"That would be nice," Collin said. He didn't feel like anything stronger. Alan sent a text message before sitting down. "Thank you for looking at Jester."

Alan grinned. "Are you kidding? I'm going to work with him myself. I've wanted a horse with his unbridled need for speed." He actually rubbed his hands together. "This is going to be great."

George shook his head. "Would you go on down and get the tea? The staff are probably overwhelmed with the guests in the house. I could also use some biscuits and maybe a scone with my tea."

"All right." Alan jumped back up and gave George a kiss before leaving the room.

"You can sure tell he wasn't raised English," Collin said.

"No. He's brash and bold and—"

"Totally amazing. Don't get me wrong for a second. I like that about him. He knows what he wants, and he goes for it without pretense or the need to parse the meaning from what he isn't saying." Collin sighed. "It makes Alan pretty special."

George leaned forward. "When they made Alan, they broke the mold." He smiled happily.

"I can tell. But I'm so tired of dating guys who find out I have a title and decide to see what they can get."

George laughed. "Like Berty?"

"You had to bring him up, didn't you?" Collin said. "I thought he was a nice guy...."

"Until you found out about his wife, two kids, and house in Leeds." George was having way too much fun.

"And let's not forget the two dogs." He shook his head. "And that's not the worst. The last man I got serious with was into latex and everything that goes with it. Now, I'm fine with whatever kink turns someone on, but don't wait until I'm naked, waiting for a guy to join me, only for him to come out in head-to-toe body latex to spring it on me." He closed his eyes. "I want a real man and not someone who knows me as the Viscount Haferton or the heir to the Earl of Doddington. All I get then are fakes and suck-ups."

"That can happen. But there are solid men out there too."

"I know. They just don't seem to cross my path."

"Then come to America with George and me," Alan said as he strode into the room with a tray. He set it on the table and sat back down. "He and I are going back to see my family for a few weeks. Mom needs some help, and I want to spend a little time at home. Mom is getting married in a few months and there's a lot for her to do, but Claude, her fiancé, is going to be traveling on business. I can introduce you around town as a friend from England. No one needs to know your title, and frankly, most people there don't care about that sort of thing. They measure a man by his actions." Alan slipped an arm around George. "That's what drew me to him. He's a good man."

"It just took you some time to see it," George added. "And yeah, you should come with us. We leave in two weeks, so there's time to get a plane ticket."

"There's room at the ranch," Alan said, "but it's a working spread."

"Collin works hard—always has," George said.

"I've been around horses and livestock all my life," Collin told Alan, excited at the prospect of getting away for a while.

Alan leaned forward. "What is your father going to say about you leaving with us for a few weeks?" It was common knowledge that though Collin was close friends with George and Alan, his father didn't like either of them. George and Alan had moved their estate forward and were on the road to profitability, while Collin's father insisted on doing things the way they had been done for years. Fortunately the family had more resources than their land holdings. But Collin's father hadn't kept up with things the way he should have, and the fact that George and Alan had their home set up as a showpiece with a garden restoration in progress and more and more tourists paying them a visit, well, it galled him. In Collin's opinion, his dad wasn't especially ambitious and spent his time being jealous of others rather than doing something to improve his lot. "You know he's going to be as stubborn as a mule."

"Then I'll have to deal with him."

Alan poured George and Collin each a cup of tea and then some coffee for himself. For a Yank, Alan made a nice cup of tea. As he sipped it, Collin tried to figure out what the hell he was going to do about dear old Dad.

"YOU AREN'T going anywhere. I need you here looking after our horses instead of running off on some holiday with the duke," Collin's father declared his study. He had a book in one hand and a glass of whisky in the other, which would have been fine if it hadn't been two in the afternoon when everyone else was working. Not Dad. He thought of himself as a man of leisure. More like a lazy ass, in Collin's opinion, which he kept to himself.

"I haven't had any time away from the estate in years. I work hard, and you know it." Harder than his father, but Collin held his tongue. "I have money of my own. I'm not asking you to pay for anything." That was something else his father didn't like. When his mother had passed two years ago, she had left everything—no inconsiderable amount—to Collin. His father had been trying to get his hands on it for some time, but Collin and his solicitor had the money tied up tight and well away from his father. "I'm an adult, and I don't need your permission to go."

His father set his book aside, and the whisky in his glass sloshed as he sat forward. "Now listen here, boy. You need to think about how you're going to continue this family. That title of yours is secondary to mine and doesn't come with anything. The earldom, my title, is attached to this estate, and it needs to continue after I'm through. You need to make sure it passes to your heirs as well. Wait." He sneered. "Your kind and those over at the dukedom don't have heirs."

Collin remained standing, hating the way his father dismissed him and his friends. "Why do you act like this?" He decided to try the direct approach. "You know the duke and his husband are good people. They helped you out last fall, and yet you talk that way."

"People like that—" his father began.

"Like what? Hard workers? People who are willing to put in the effort?" Collin met his father's steely gaze, expecting a blowup. "You should be ashamed of how you talk about them and about me. I'm your son."

His father glared at him. "There are times I wonder about that."

Collin could feel the heat rising in his cheeks. "Really? You're saying that Mom had an affair? Really? And she found someone as pale and round-faced as you are to screw around with?" He'd always wondered why his mother had stayed with his father. The man had few redeeming qualities.

"I just meant…," he blustered, and for a second Collin thought he might have seen the first hint that his father knew he'd gone too far—something rare in the man.

"I know what you were saying. That I don't measure up and that you wanted someone different for a son. Maybe you wanted someone who was straight, or maybe a kid who is as useless and lazy as you." He had had enough of his father's picking, controlling attitude. "I'll leave in two weeks and will be away for a fortnight. I have a right, and I'm perfectly free to go."

"Fine," his father snapped. "But I expect something in return."

Collin chuckled. "Like what? You forget that I don't owe you anything. My title has been registered with Debrett's, so trying to remove it would cause talk. In fact, anything you do will cause talk, and I know you don't want that." His father wasn't exactly in favor with any of the local gentry, so a scandal would only push him further to the edges of local society, and that would hurt. "Just stop, Father. You don't get to control me or run my life."

To Collin's surprise, his father picked up his book once more and just shook his head. "Fine. You go to America with your friends." The way he said it made Collin wonder what he thought he was up to. But Collin wasn't going to stick around to try to puzzle out the many wavering paths of his father's mind. That was a job that would stymie a team of psychoanalysts.

"I'll make sure everything is seen to and let you know the exact dates I'll be gone." He left the room and then placed a call to George, who made flight arrangements for him, and Collin was all set. He hung up the phone and wondered why he was so excited. He had just volunteered to go to America and spend two weeks on a ranch. Yes, he worked with horses, but he knew very little about being a cowboy.

Still, it was a chance to get away from his father and Westworth and all the problems his father seemed intent on ignoring. Perhaps with him gone, the earl would have to get up off his posterior and do something. Collin still wondered what his father had up his sleeve, but he put the thoughts aside.

His phone rang, and Collin answered it right away. "What's up?" he asked Riley, his best friend from school.

"I was calling to see if you wanted to hit the pub tonight." Riley always had enough energy for three people. His mother worked on George's estate and had since Riley was a kid. Riley was whip-smart, and George's father had helped him get into some of the best schools, which was where Collin had met him.

"Sure. I can meet you." He checked the time. "Hook and Castle in an hour?"

"Sounds good," Riley said just as Collin's father entered the room. He fixed Collin with a glare. He didn't like Riley either. Collin was starting to think his father hated everyone in Collin's life. Not that it mattered.

"Yes, it does," he said gently. "I'll meet you at the pub, and I can tell you all about my upcoming trip to America." He held his father's gaze, watching that little vein on his forehead.

"You're leaving?" Riley asked, aghast.

"Just for two weeks. I'm traveling with the duke and Alan, and I'll be spending the time on a ranch there." He waited until his father left the room again before smiling.

"I take it that little scene was for your father. Are you really going?" Riley knew the workings of his relationship with his father better than Collin did sometimes.

"Yeah. I think it's time I try to build a life of my own somehow, and I'm not going to do it here. My father is getting even worse."

"The gay thing?" Riley asked.

"And that 'carry on the family line' thing," he added. "I'm tired of all of it. Enough is enough, so I'm leaving the country for a while."

Riley sighed. "I wish I could go. I'd love to find me a cowboy and ride him over the range." Collin snickered at Riley's joke. Or maybe he was serious. It was sometimes hard to tell. "I'll still be here trying to get this spirit shop of mine up and running, and you'll be over in America finding cowboys to ride."

Collin should be so lucky.

CHAPTER 2

TIMOTHY "TANK" Rogers sat on the porch of his ranch house, looking over his own little kingdom—and that was how he thought of it. After eight years in service to his country, he had returned home with a bum leg that still ached sometimes, to a father who was so ill he could barely stand.

Tank had nursed his dad, but all he could do was keep him comfortable those last days. Cancer was a bitch from hell. He grieved by spending the next two years working his ass off to stave off foreclosure and put the ranch back in shape. Now his place was prosperous. One thing Tank had learned in the service was that he couldn't do it alone, and with the help of good neighbors, he had seen himself and his people through the darkest of times.

He sipped his tea, ice cubes tinkling in the glass, condensation dripping onto his shirt. Tank paid it no mind. There were still things to do, but he needed a break to rest his aching leg.

Tank sat forward as an old but familiar car turned into his drive. "Chip," he said when his neighbor's youngest son got out. Tank would know him anywhere. Chip was cute, and Tank always had an eye out for cute. He was also way off-limits: too young, his neighbor's boy, and Chip was straight and dating one of the girls in town. Not that Tank would ever allow himself to get serious about the kid anyway. His daddy always told him not to shit where he ate, and Chip Justice was way too close to home. Still, he wasn't dead, and there was no harm in looking.

"Hey, Tank." Chip closed the car door and ambled up toward the porch.

"You want some tea?" He was about to get up when Chip sat down.

"No, thanks. Besides, I know where it is if I need any." He smiled that bright, open grin he always had. Chip was a ray of sunshine in what could otherwise be a dark and harsh world. Tank hoped the world let him stay that way. "Mama wanted me to stop by on my way home from work." He never slowed down. In addition to the ranch, Chip used to work at a store in town, but now he assisted John Hasper, one of the local vets, during the summer.

"First, why don't you tell me why you keep looking down at your shoes?"

The smile slid away, and the sparkle in those eyes flashed out in a second. "Someone brought in some dogs they found out north of town. They were in bad shape. Three of the young ones died while I held them. I've seen animals die before, and I know it happens, but they were just puppies. The vet said that the fleas had almost drained them dry."

"You helped save the others, right?" Tank asked, and Chip nodded. "Then think on that. The other dogs are here and have a chance because of you."

"Yeah," Chip breathed. "But all of them need homes, and they ain't ranch dogs. They're small. The mama isn't much more than ten pounds, and the pups were tiny. But they're all cute little things."

"And your mother isn't going to let you bring home any more dogs." Tank knew that for sure. The Justice ranch already had a menagerie of Chip's foundlings. "You tell Doc that I'll take the dogs if they need homes." Hell, he needed some company around the house, and dogs were a lot easier to get along with than people. "Now, what did your mama want?"

"Next week, Alan and George are coming back for a visit. Mama is in a real dither because she wants the visit to go well, but Alan called to say that they're bringing a friend with them. The house is going to be really full, and Mama doesn't want to put this Collin out in the bunkhouse with the men."

Tank sipped from his glass. "Why not?"

"For one thing, he's a guest, and for another, he's a viscount, the son of one of Alan and George's neighbors, and Mama wants to make a good impression. Mama wanted me to ask you if Collin could stay here with you. She said to tell you she would be doing the cooking." Chip sat back in his chair.

Tank had to admit that was an enticement. Chip's mother was an amazing cook, and the thought of home-cooked meals was almost enough to get him to agree. But Tank was used to being alone, and he didn't need someone else in his house.

"I know it's a lot to ask. I told Mama that I could move the furniture around and make room for Collin in the office or something. But you know her."

Tank found himself nodding. "Your mama is a kind lady, and she helps out everyone. So if she needs me to put up this Viscount Collin while he's here, then you tell her yes. Anything to get me some of her biscuits and gravy." If she was going to be cooking, he might as well put in for some of his favorites. Maureen Justice was one of those people who asked very little and gave a lot to others, so even though the thought of having someone in his house for a few weeks made him want to scratch his skin off, he smiled and agreed.

"I'll be sure to tell her, and thank you." Chip smiled again. "For taking the dogs, and for letting this viscount guy stay here."

"Have you met him?" Tank asked.

"I think I might have when I visited Alan and George last summer. I spent a lot of my time out in the stables with the horses and the folks who worked there."

Tank clapped Chip on the shoulder. "Of course you did. Anyone would. Who needs fancy people who hide behind bowing, scraping, titles, and 'yes, my lord'?"

Chip shrugged. "It wasn't like that. George is a duke and he has an estate and stuff, but he's a great guy and he doesn't act that way or expect his people to bow and scrape. The people who work for him have various ways of addressing him, mainly because they respect him, and I think they feel the same way about Alan. I thought like you did and was kind of intimidated, but it's a respect sort of thing. I know you understand that."

"Does this viscount expect us to use his title?"

"Nope. George says that we are to call him Collin. His father's an earl who Alan says is a real piece of work." Chip jumped to his feet. "I got to go or Mama is going to start to wonder where I am, and there are still chores to get done."

Tank finished his tea and stood as well, working the stiffness out of his leg. "There's always work on a ranch."

"George made it clear to Mama that Collin will be here to help out. Alan says he knows we have working ranches, and he is supposed to be good with horses."

"We can always use help." Tank took off his hat to let the breeze reach his hairless head. He wasn't sure how this Collin fellow was going to fare after a day of real ranch work, but he figured they'd all find out.

"THAT'S IT, girl," Tank said softly as he stroked her nose. "You're going to be fine. Just give yourself a break." He sat on a bale of hay, stroking the rat terrier mama, her two remaining pups playing in the box around her. Sheba was cute and seemed taken with him, but the poor thing was jumpy, like she expected some predator to come up and devour her at any minute. "I'm here, and I ain't going to let nothing happen to you." He'd brought her out to the barn so she wouldn't be alone, but now he wondered if that was a good idea.

Sheba began to bark, sharply and as loud as her little body could muster. She stood rigid, a pup on each side.

"Tank?"

"It's Chip," Tank told the silly girl, who began wagging her tail as soon as she saw him.

Chip hurried over and lifted Sheba in his hands, holding her to his chest. "What's all that noise for?" he asked her, petting gently. Tank lifted and caressed each of the still-tiny pups. "Alan, George, and Collin are arriving today. I expect them in an hour or so."

"Your mama texted," Tank said. "Let's get these guys in the house. I thought she'd be calmer if I stayed close, but it isn't working."

"She needs predictability," Chip said. "They got these dog beds at the clinic. I'll bring you one. That way she can have her own space." He rocked slowly, and Sheba seemed much happier.

Tank led the way to the house, where Chip set down Sheba and Tank set down Liza and Danny. Tank was still trying to find homes for them, but for now, his little doggie family seemed happy. "I came by to make sure you were ready for guests. And before you say anything, Mama insisted. She wants to make sure that Collin isn't too much of a problem for you."

"Everything is fine. I cleaned and put fresh sheets on the bed and everything." He wasn't sure how he felt that Maureen thought she needed to check up on him, though Tank wasn't exactly the "hosting a houseguest" type. "Should I have gotten mints to put on his pillow?"

Chip patted his shoulder. "No, and I'm sorry about all this. I offered to give up my room and stay in the bunkhouse."

Tank looked around the house he had grown up in, the one that his grandfather had built for an entire family rather than just for him. He had three unused bedrooms in the place, so if Collin wanted, he could take his pick. "This is fine." He ran a critical eye over his living room and wondered what Viscount What's-His-Name would think of his old, mismatched furniture.

Sheba ran in, leaped up on the sofa, and got comfortable, blinking her big eyes at him, the definition of cuteness.

"Well, thank you again for doing this. Mom says that dinner will be in two hours, and we'll see you then." Chip said goodbye and hurried out.

Tank got out the broom, vacuum, and duster and started cleaning the house all over again.

TANK CLUNG to the bouquet of flowers he'd brought for Maureen as he got out of his truck and walked slowly up to the front door. He knocked, and Alan opened it and pulled him into a hug. "It's good to see you, man." He thumped Tank on the back and stepped away. "Come on in. Everyone is in the kitchen talking." He waited and closed the door, motioning Tank through.

The scent from the kitchen pulled him forward. Tank stepped in and stopped. George sat at the table with a cup of tea. He stood, and they shook hands. Tank had met him briefly before, but they hadn't had a chance to talk much.

The man next to him stood.

"Collin, this is Timothy," Alan said.

"But everyone calls me Tank." His voice sounded different to him, and he hoped to hell it didn't crack like a teenager's. He'd been calm under fire multiple times, but Collin left him unsure of what to say. He was handsome and almost regal. "You're the Viscount Something-or-Other?"

"Yes. I have a title, but just call me Collin, okay?" He seemed really subdued, and his voice was quiet. Tank leaned closer to hear him. "I'm a friend of George and Alan's." He smiled beautifully, and all Tank could do was nod. He straightened up and shook the offered hand.

"It's good to meet you," Tank said, forcing his control back into place. He had been trained to handle any situation, and the fact that the ground under his feet seemed to have turned to quicksand from awe and sheer attraction to the sexy redhead had him falling back onto old protocols: stay cool, think, and be on guard. In this case, he decided to redirect and give the flowers he'd brought to Maureen.

"Did you grow these?" she asked before sniffing them.

"I did. Mama always had a flower garden, so last year I found where hers had been and planted one of my own." It might have seemed like a waste of time and effort to some people, but for Tank it made it seem like his own mama was a little closer to him, even if he would never tell anyone that, even on threat of death. Showing weakness only let others get close enough to hurt you.

"They're beautiful." She kissed Tank on the cheek before going to put them in water. She did that sometimes, and Tank never knew what to do with it. He simply smiled a little and tried not to blush. "Sit down and get off your feet. Dinner will be ready in about fifteen minutes."

Tank pulled out a chair and sat, listening as the others talked about the trip and what a pain travel was. "Do you tell people you're a duke?" Chip asked. "I bet you can get better seats and stuff."

Alan snickered. "There was that British Airways gate attendant who wasn't very cooperative at Heathrow." He bumped George's shoulder like he was sharing a big secret, and the upright, proper-posture duke beamed back at him like Alan hung the moon.

"Let's not get into that," George said.

Alan leaned forward, making it clear he was going to tell the story regardless of what George thought. "You'd have thought she was the queen herself. People were lined up everywhere and they needed help, and all she did was talk to one of the maintenance guys. George gets out of the queue and walks up to the counter. She pauses her conversation to glare at George. He pulled out his wallet and showed her his identification. She sneered and then saw the crest and the title and paled. I thought she was going to pass out."

"What did you do?" Chip asked. "Did you tell her off?"

"I didn't say a word," George said.

Alan snickered. "No, he didn't. But she about wet herself and snapped to. George waited his turn in the queue, and by the time we got up to the front of the line, we had the best seats on the plane."

"You got an upgrade?"

"No. I had already paid for premium seats, but we got changed to better ones, and she was able to put us together."

"Did Collin get to sit with you?"

Collin shook his head. "I had a seat in the regular cabin. It was all that was available."

Maureen set a glass of iced tea in front of him, and Tank sipped it, grateful for something to do. He wasn't much of a conversationalist, so he let the others do the talking and mostly listened and kept glancing at Collin.

The man intrigued him, but that didn't really matter. Collin could have made a huge deal about where he'd been seated, but he downplayed it, like anyone else. He was here for two weeks, and that was all. Collin was also a guest of the Justices. On top of that, Tank didn't need anyone complicating his life, no matter that the sight of the guy made his blood run hotter. He had already had more of that than he needed for as long as he lived.

Maureen brought dinner to the table: a beef roast, potatoes, fresh vegetables, and to top it off, one of her fresh berry pies. The entire room filled with a home-cooked scent that Tank hadn't experienced in a long time. He'd never been much of a cook, though he was getting better at it now that he had to. His dad had been amazing in the kitchen, and so had his mom.

Tank turned toward where Maureen was getting the second pie, and he could remember his parents bringing dinner to the table while he watched and waited, his belly rumbling just the way it did now.

"Thank you," Tank said to Maureen when she passed him a plate. His instinct was to tuck right in, but he watched as the others waited for everyone to be served. Then, once Maureen sat down, he began to eat.

"Have you been on your ranch for long?" Collin asked from next to him.

"All my life," Tank answered. "My grandparents started the place, and they left it to my father, who left it to me." Look at him being social.

"Like my home. It was built by the third earl, and the family has lived there since." Collin smiled as he talked about it.

"How many earls have there been?" he asked, more to give Collin something to talk about than anything. He had a nice voice.

"My father is the eighth Earl of Doddington. I'll be the ninth, and after that I'm not sure who will follow me."

"I thought you were a viscount or something. You won't stay that?"

Collin set down his fork. "The viscount title is a secondary one. Before I was born, my father was the Viscount Haferton and Earl of Doddington. Now he's still the earl, and I'm the viscount. When he dies, I'll be both until I have a son, which my father is pressuring me to do."

Chip leaned over the table. "But... how are you going to do that?" He glanced at Alan and then at George in confusion.

"Well, I won't put some woman, especially one my father might think is suitable, through that kind of lie. I haven't figured out how exactly I'm going to have a child, but I will." The determination in Collin's voice set something ablaze in Tank that he tried to douse, but he could feel his cheeks heating. Collin must be gay! The idea gave Tank a feeling he dared not name as hope. "I have to keep the line going, but I won't hurt anyone in the process."

Tank lifted his gaze to Collin. "That's a very cowboy attitude." The others nodded, and Tank went back to his dinner, trying not to show the excitement that had his belly fluttering. Still, just because Collin was gay didn't mean he would be interested in Tank. It was better and safer to keep his feelings to himself.

CHAPTER 3

COLLIN WASN'T sure what to make of Tank. He tried talking to him but got only short answers to his questions. After dinner, everyone moved into the living room, and Collin sat next to Tank to engage him in conversation. He was supposed to be spending the next two weeks staying at his house, and it was going to be a long visit if Tank was the strong, silent type.

Chip managed to get Tank to talk, but the two of them chatted about feed stores and chores that needed to be done. "Did you ever ride rodeo?" Collin asked Tank, trying to find something to talk about. "I watched it on the telly a few years ago. I thought it pretty amazing how men could ride those animals."

"I was too tall," Tank said, and Collin waited to see if he would continue. "Alan rode rodeo for a time, if I remember. He was pretty good. It wasn't for me, so I became a soldier for a while." He drank some more of his tea, and it seemed that was all Collin was going to get.

Collin wondered what Tank might have seen during that period, but kept his curiosity to himself. His experience was that most people didn't want to talk about those times. "Are there rodeos here?" he asked, changing the subject.

"Yeah. There's one next week up in Creekwood," Chip said. "You should go. Maybe Tank could take you up there to see it." Collin got the idea that Chip was just being himself, but it seemed by the scowl he got from Tank that it wasn't likely that would be happening. The guy was huge, with muscles bulging out of his shirt. Tank could have looked mean—well, he actually did in some ways, especially with the bald head—but Collin wasn't sure if he actually was or not. His instincts were conflicted, but he kept going back to the fact that Alan's mother seemed to like him, so he couldn't really be bad.

"That would be fun," George offered. "I can see about getting us all tickets, and we could look at making a day of it." Tank didn't say anything, but Collin was grateful for George's effort.

"You boys have all traveled a long way and have to be tired."

"Yeah, and I need to get up early for chores," Tank said flatly. Collin took that as his cue that it was time for them to leave.

"You come for breakfast in the morning," Maureen told Tank. "I'm making the french toast that you liked so much when you were here for Easter brunch." She hugged Tank and Collin too. Then Tank said goodbye, and Collin followed him out into the night, wondering just what he was getting himself in for.

"How FAR away is your ranch?" Collin asked as Tank drove.

"Not far," he answered and kept driving. Collin was starting to wonder if they were going to end up in the next state, but then Tank turned in and pulled up near a huge home, low to the ground and a single story. In the front porch lights, he saw some weathered wood.

"Thank you for letting me stay," Collin said, and Tank hummed something that Collin didn't understand.

"Go on and take your bags inside. Your room is the first one on the right down the hall. I got some things to see to." He trundled off toward the barn, and Collin stood outside. Cows lowed nearby, and in the distance, a howl carried over the land on the breeze. Collin picked up his suitcase and hurried up to the door to let himself in.

Three intense barks greeted him in the dimness. Collin started and fumbled for a light switch, then turned on an overhead light. He snickered as the small dog and two puppies stood rigidly in front of him, barking their heads off.

"Oh my God." Collin smiled. He would have expected Tank to have a dog as big as he was, and instead, they were these cute little beauties. "I'm Collin, and you can stop barking." He knelt down and held out his hand. The larger dog sniffed him and then licked his hand before coming forward. He gently stroked her head, and then the others followed suit, climbing over each other for attention. "Aren't you sweet?" He petted them all before standing up. He found the hall and took his bag to the room Tank had indicated.

All three dogs followed him, the bigger one jumping on the bed while the other two whined and tried to get up. Collin put them next to her, and the three of them formed a little doggie pile, curling up together.

Collin opened his suitcase and unpacked, hanging things up in the closet. He wondered what he should do. Tank seemed to have escaped to the barn, and Collin had no idea what time to expect him inside. He was tired after all the travel, so he changed into sleep clothes and lay on the bed with a book. The dogs all nuzzled close, and soon the words muddled in his head. Collin set the book aside and closed his eyes. The house was quiet and the air was fresh. He didn't mean to fall asleep, but the last thing he remembered was one of the pups climbing onto his chest.

He woke at some point in the night. The house was dark, the dogs were gone, and he'd been covered by a blanket. He checked the time—a little after four in the morning—and then rolled over, closing his eyes once more. The bed was soft enough and the blanket the right weight that he was warm, but not too warm.

The scent of coffee pulled him awake. Collin sat up, stretching and yawning as he rubbed his eyes, surprised at how long he slept. He felt scruffy and needed to wash off the travel, but his nose led him to the kitchen, where he found the coffee pot but an otherwise empty house. As soon as he sat, the dogs raced over, the two pups practically rolling over each other in their haste. Collin gave all of them some attention and finished his coffee before returning to the bedroom. He changed clothes and used the bathroom to freshen up a little before deciding he should find his host.

Tank was out in the yard, a horse on a training lead. It seemed like he was trying to build trust, especially with how softly he spoke to the horse. "Morning," Collin called gently.

"Don't move," Tank said immediately, and Collin leaned against the fence, watching as Tank worked the skittish horse. Tank spoke softly enough that Collin couldn't hear the words, but the horse obviously could. Finally, Tank stopped and led the horse over.

"What happened to her?" Collin asked, using the tone he would at home for a horse who had been frightened.

Tank kept her away from the fence. "Someone terrorized the poor thing." He rubbed her nose, and the horse started, but Tank continued, and she calmed once she realized he wasn't going to hurt her.

"I see." Collin said softly. "You're a pretty girl, though," he said, addressing the horse, making sure she saw him. "Yes, you are." Her ears twitched, and she took a step closer. "Tank will never hurt you, so you can calm down. That's it." She took another step forward, and Collin spoke even softer, letting his voice soothe her. He wasn't sure if this was what Tank wanted, but he didn't move her away, so Collin kept talking until the chestnut beauty came even nearer. Slowly Collin reached out, letting her see his hands before stroking her neck.

"You've done this before," Tank said very softly.

"Yes. My father had a string of horses, and there was one like this pretty girl. He bought her at auction and got her for a pittance. He didn't know what was wrong with her until he got her home and the tranquilizers wore off. She about tore the place apart. But I got her calm." Collin smiled. "She wasn't as pretty as this beauty, but she was a good horse… for me. Belle hated my father." That gave him a small smile. "She had good taste." His little joke was met with a flat reaction.

"Rocket here was abused. The county took her away from her owners, along with eight other horses. They had been mistreated for quite some time." Tank treated her so gently, it was almost surprising, given how gruff he seemed to be. "I got her a month ago, and you're the first person, 'sides me, that she's let get close to her." Tank clicked his tongue and slowly led her away while Collin wondered if he'd actually gotten a compliment from the quiet loner.

Collin watched Tank go, his footsteps raising tiny clouds of dust, tight jeans encasing his thick legs and bum. And what a bum it was. His back widened to broad shoulders. This was definitely a man Collin wouldn't want to meet in a dark alley, and yet in the light of day, there was a sheen of vulnerability around him, like this silence and gruff demeanor were covering for something. Of course, that could be Collin's imagination. Still, he stayed where he was, shifting his attention to the other horses once it seemed like Tank might turn back. He didn't want to be caught staring. Who knew how Tank would react?

He sighed and wondered what he'd gotten himself into. Collin had battled his father and accepted whatever consequences the vindictive old coot would decide to dish out so he could come here. Maybe he had this ridiculous fantasy that guys like Alan were lined up looking for someone like him, and he'd just have to go down the line to choose the model he wanted. That was stupid.

He pushed away from the fence. His phone vibrated with a message from George to say that breakfast was on in ten minutes, so Collin went to find Tank.

"What are you doing?" Collin asked as he entered the barn. Tank had a horse in crossties and was working on a foot. "Shouldn't the vet be doing that?"

Tank looked up at him like he was crazy. "I been cleaning and caring for horses' hooves since I was twelve." He flicked the tool, and a stone arced through the air to the floor. "That's better, isn't it, boy." He checked over the hoof and then set it down. "I'm going to give you some extra oats for that because you were good." He patted the gelding's neck and undid the ties, then moved him back to the stall.

"Breakfast is in a few minutes," Collin said as Tank closed the stall door. Tank nodded, watching him intently, like he might want to ask something. "Go ahead."

"Do you really have a vet do the simplest things?" Tank asked. "You got that much money?"

"We don't have loads of it, no. We have land and the estate, which generate income. But we don't waste it." Unless you counted his father and the fact that he had no sense at all.

"Out here we do for ourselves as much as possible," Tank explained. "The vet will come, but he covers maybe a thousand square miles. I could call him for something simple like that stone, but then another ranch might need him for a troubled birth fifty miles away and he wouldn't get there in time." He strode toward the house, and Collin followed, wondering if he had just been smacked down. He decided that had simply been an explanation of life here and a different take on things.

Collin washed up and rode with Tank to Maureen's, where a huge, heaping breakfast awaited them. The others settled at the table now that they had arrived. He took a couple of pieces of french toast and a few pieces of bacon as well as some eggs and slowly began to eat. Without asking, Tank added more bacon and eggs to his plate, as well as two pieces of sausage.

"What am I supposed to do with all that?" It was a mountainous amount of food. Collin had never eaten that much at one sitting in his life.

"You'll need it," Tank said as he tucked right in.

"What I'll do is explode," he retorted, and the cowboys all chuckled.

"We're going over to Tank's today. One of the water retention ponds needs the intake feed cleaned out. It's going to be a hot, heavy job, so eat up," Alan said. "You're going to need all your energy." He had that serious look of his, so Collin ate all he could, but he still left a piece of sausage. He finished all the bacon because, dang, that stuff was good.

ONCE THEY were in the yard, Tank plopped a hat onto Collin's head. "You can use it," he gruffed and headed over to an ATV.

"You'll need these as well, and this." George tossed him gloves and a long-sleeved shirt. "The sun is fierce, so you'll burn if you don't cover up. Chip is driving the truck over with the tools. You go get on behind Tank, and he'll drive you over."

Collin turned to where Tank waited and wondered if there would be room for him. George got on behind Alan, slipping his arms around his waist, and then Alan took off. As Collin hopped onto the ATV behind him, he hoped Tank didn't dump him somewhere. Tank scooted up a little, and once Collin put his arms around Tank and got a feel for his flat, hard belly, they started out, and all Collin could concentrate on was not falling off.

The ride was bumpy and fast. They zoomed over the land, through pastures and paddock gates. "Always leave a gate the way you found it," Tank told him as they passed through one, and he had Collin close it. Then they continued on across a huge open pasture to what looked like a small lake glistening in the sun.

Collin got off and joined the others once Tank had dismounted.

"See the mud around the edge? That used to be the level of the water," Alan explained. "Grab a shovel from the back of the truck and follow Tank. He'll show us what needs to be done."

Collin pulled on his gloves and got a shovel while other guys from the ranches arrived. Then he followed the others to a dry indentation in the ground. "The sides seem to have fallen in," he told George. "They probably weren't reinforced properly, and the water washed them away." Collin continued up the embankment with Tank behind him. "What's with those stones over there?" he asked, pointing to a couple of rock piles to the side of the field.

"They were part of an original house that was here a long time ago. We lost it in a storm in the fifties, and we left the stone. We can use it to reinforce the banks. Have a couple people load them up and bring them over."

"Then once we re-dig the channel, we can line it with the rock and it will be more stable," Collin added.

Tank nodded, and two of the men unloaded the equipment and rode off with Chip. The others began digging to deepen the channel, starting at the pond, while Collin made sure the slope was right. This was his element. He had studied hydrology in school, so he knew the basics. In a country where it rained a lot, managing the flow of water was a big deal.

When the guys arrived with the stone, he explained how to lay it, with the large pieces on the bottom and smaller ones on top. "Put the ones this size along the base of the sides." He showed them how to do it, and the men got to the heavy work. Collin then helped with the digging.

Within an hour, he understood the need for the huge breakfast. He had also never been so sweaty and hot in his life. His shirt was soaked through, plastered to his skin, and so was Tank's, giving Collin a good view of the ridges on his belly and the way his large nipples peaked the fabric.

As they got closer to the water source, the main earthen dam was the final obstacle. "We need to get all the rock laid before we remove this," Collin instructed.

"All hands to the rock," Tank bellowed, and they made short work of getting everything hauled over and placed. Then Alan began digging away at the top of the berm.

"No, start farther back," Collin explained. "We want as little of that debris as possible to flow back up the channel. So make it as thin as we can, and then the water will do the rest." He dug in, making a hole just up from the obstruction. Mud and dirt filled every crease, and then the water took what remained and flowed down. The remaining dirt filled in his hole, and soon the water ran clear up to Tank's retention pond. "Now fill in the rest of the rock in this area."

Everyone chipped in to get the last part done. "Drinks at Clancey's are on Tank," Alan declared as he clapped Tank on the shoulder.

"You all did good, and I thank you." Tank turned to Collin with a smile. "All of you." Everyone gathered up the tools and loaded the back of the truck. Then Collin climbed up behind Tank and they rode back to the ranch house, where Maureen had a heaping table of food set up on the back patio ready for what Collin could only describe as the biggest meal of his life—and this time he understood why.

"ARE YOU ready to go?" Alan asked as he strode into Tank's living room.

"You go. I have things to do." Tank handed Alan a credit card. "You know I'm not... social."

Collin watched as the two men stared at each other. "This isn't social. It's a thank-you for everyone who helped you. You know that, and you need to be the one who says it." Alan wasn't angry or upset, just firm, and Tank nodded. He took back his card and went down the hall, where he closed his bedroom door. Collin wondered if Tank was okay and what had happened to him. This wasn't some sort of social anxiety thing; it was more than that. He turned to Alan, who shrugged like he had no idea what was going on either.

Collin figured Tank would return in clean jeans and a fresh flannel shirt, but he was so wrong. Black pants, white shirt open at the collar with a hint of tan skin, fresh, almost white hat with feathered decoration, and alligator boots that practically sparkled. He was a spectacle, and Collin's mouth went dry. "Are we going?"

"Yes," George said, and Alan tossed him the keys. They all left the house and got into George's rented SUV, heading for town.

Clancey's seemed like a cowboy bar straight out of the movies. There were trophies mounted on the walls, neon beer signs, and rows of plank wood tables with benches crowded with people. Music played over it all, adding to the din. The only thing missing was the smoke, for which Collin was grateful. They found a table at the far end of the room.

"Looking spiffy, boss," one of the hands said. Tank nodded and sat down at the end of the table. He got a round of beer for everyone, and they all settled in and ordered food, laughing and talking up a storm.

"Is it always like this?' Collin asked George, who was sitting next to him.

"Pretty much. Ranches are sort of like a family. It's a hard life with a lot of work, like today, so time off is precious. Tonight is kind of special, and everyone is behaving themselves because Tank is here. He never comes out."

Collin leaned closer. "Is this a gay cowboy bar?" He'd heard of those.

George shook his head. "But Alan and I will probably dance. It's okay. Clancey doesn't take crap from anyone, and he's made it clear that if they can't accept folks for who they are, then they know where the door is." George gestured to the far side of the bar, where the biggest man Collin had ever seen stood, looking over the proceedings. The server took orders, but Collin was still full from dinner, so he got a dark beer, sipped it, and watched people.

The band started playing about ten, and the room jumped into action. "Do you wanna dance?" a man asked Collin with a smile. "I'm Teddy. I work over at the North Spike." He seemed pleasant, so Collin nodded and let Teddy teach him the steps, which didn't take long. "You're really cute."

"Thanks," Collin said as the cowboy drew him closer. He smelled good, like fresh hay and the outdoors. He was sexy and seemed nice enough. As they danced, Collin relaxed and went with the music, allowing himself to have a good time, even smiling at Teddy. Maybe coming here had been a good decision.

CHAPTER 4

TANK COULDN'T take his eyes off Collin and Teddy, as if staring at them would make them get the idea that he was fuming inside. He knew he had no right to be, so he grabbed a chicken wing out of the nearby basket to give his hands something to do. He ate without thinking about it.

"If you stare any harder, you're going to bore a hole in the other wall," Alan said from next to him.

Tank growled and reached for another wing, but found an empty basket. He didn't say anything because that would only give Alan's comment weight, and that was the last thing he wanted.

"Come on. I can tell you like the guy," Alan said. "You watch him all the time."

"So he don't screw anything up," Tank argued.

"Right, and dancing with Teddy is going to hurt anything?" Alan teased. "You wore your best clothes because Collin was going to be here and you wanted to impress him."

Sometimes Alan saw way too damned much. "You said I needed to thank the guys."

"You could have done that in a shirt and jeans, not your 'look at me, I'm a peacock' clothes and a hat and boots that put everyone else's to shame. I've known you too long." Alan nudged his shoulder. "If you're interested in Collin, then you best stake your claim, or else Teddy is going to have him lassoed and branded as his own. And you know you don't steal from another cowboy."

Tank hadn't taken his eyes off the pair. "It don't matter."

"That's bullshit, and you know it." Alan jabbed him again. "Now get your sorry ass off that seat and go over there and cut in." Alan stood himself and took George by the hand, then dragged him to the floor.

The truth was that Tank wanted what the two of them had, but he didn't think it was in the cards for him. It never had been. He was convinced that he was one of those guys who was meant to be alone. It was safer for him—and, well, everyone else, as far as Tank was concerned. Still, his insides churned. Damn it all, he had seen a hell of a lot when he was in the Army, and he was damned well not going to chicken out over some guy.

Tank pushed himself up and strode over to Teddy. "I'd like a dance, if you don't mind." He met Teddy's gaze, and the kid paled a little before stepping back. "Is that okay?" he asked Collin before taking him in his arms and guiding him across the dance floor.

"You didn't have to scare Teddy half to death," Collin said. "And you didn't have to make a huge production about asking me to dance. I would have."

"I didn't. I just cut in. It's a thing here," he explained as he twirled Collin in his arms. The man moved like a dream, and Tank had to remind himself that couldn't get too carried away.

"I see," Collin said with an adorably wicked smile as the song came to an end. Most people applauded, but Tank held Collin still, waiting for the next number to begin. "So if that cute cowboy over there were to ask me to dance, you'd step back and let him cut in?"

Tank growled, and Collin chuckled.

"I didn't think so. You enjoyed intimidating Teddy with all this, didn't you?" The mirth in his eyes was priceless. Tank picked up the pace as the next song began, moving more quickly to the up-tempo beat. "Where did you learn to dance?"

"My mama," Tank answered. "She told me that every young man needed to know how to dance if he was ever going to be able to get first pick of a wife. She died without ever knowing that I would never have a wife. But she felt strongly about such things, so she taught me how to dance. She and Daddy came here every Saturday night to eat and dance, and when I was a teenager, I came along. Where did you learn?" Tank realized that he was talking a lot more than he normally did, but it wasn't every day that he danced with someone, and Mama had told him that talking to your dance partner was polite.

"My mother arranged for me to have classes in the gentlemanly arts, as she put it. I was taught how to dance, eat properly, address all levels of nobility, bow appropriately, and how to behave in any situation. This was all drilled into me before the age of ten, when I was sent to school at Harrow. Somehow it didn't cover working as a ranch hand or dancing in a cowboy bar." Collin moved gracefully and effortlessly until the song ended.

Collin seemed unsure if he wanted to continue, but Tank tugged him closer when the music slowed. "Is something wrong?"

"In my world, if you dance with someone for three consecutive songs, that's the equivalent of a proposal of marriage." Collin met his gaze with a hard seriousness, and Tank faltered and nearly stepped on Collin's toes. "God, I really got you there, didn't I?"

Tank relaxed. "You did."

"And you seem to have staked your claim now. All the others in the room are watching us… or probably you."

Tank shook his head. "They're watching you. Everyone already knows me." He swayed to the music, and Collin rested his head on Tank's upper chest.

"That's okay, then."

Tank nearly stumbled. "You don't mind being the center of attention?" He had always hated it.

"Why do you think I had all those lessons? I'm a viscount, and eventually I'll be the earl. I've been the center of attention since I was a child. George and I were both raised the same way. As the son of a duke, he garnered even more attention than I did, and that meant that he had to be even more perfect or the talk would swirl everywhere, and that was never tolerated."

Tank understood plenty about talk. He'd been the object of a lot of it over the years. "People talk about me."

Collin glanced around with a scowl. "Why? Because you're a grumpy old bear living alone on a ranch?" Damn, that wicked smile was back. "A man has the right to live his life the way he wants to." That was a sentiment that Tank hadn't expected.

"Is that why you're here?" He turned Collin halfway, his arms around his waist as they sashayed in a circle with the other dancers.

"In part. My father wants me to live the life that he wants, and I'm fighting him on it." The music came to an end, and Collin shook his head slightly. Then he stepped back and gave Tank a little bow. "You, sir, are a fine dancer, and I'd waltz around the floor with you anytime." Then he returned to the table, sat next to George and Alan, and took a gulp of his beer.

Tank stood alone on the floor, wondering what the hell had just happened.

Alan motioned him over, and when he approached the table, Alan handed him a beer. "I think you both need something to drink."

Tank downed the contents of the glass and leaned forward to glance at Collin, who looked back at him with a smile. Okay, so maybe things weren't as bad as Tank had thought. His racing heart calmed a little, and he ordered another beer, determined to drink this one more slowly.

An hour or so later, he was ready to go home. "Maybe I should go back to the house and check on the pups," Tank proposed. He had done his duty to the guys who helped him. He'd fed and watered all of them, and they were now on to carousing and carrying on.

Alan and George nodded and finished their beers. "Collin, are you ready to go?" Alan asked.

Collin grinned. "I was thinking I'd see if I could go find Teddy. Maybe he's still interested in a dance or two." Wicked—the man was that through and through. Then Collin got up and came over to Tank. "Maybe you'd take me for another spin before we go home, cowboy?" Collin held out his hand. Tank took it and led Collin to the dance floor.

The music was hopping, and so did they. Collin kept up beautifully, and a few other couples turned to watch. Tank paid them no mind. He had Collin in his arms, and the way that man looked at him made Tank want things he knew he shouldn't. No matter how many times he danced with him or looked into Collin's eyes, Tank knew he was only here for a few weeks. And besides, Tank could let himself have a little fun, but he was destined to be alone. It was just the way of the world and his lot in life. Experience had taught him that, and there was no changing it.

The music came to an end, and once more Collin gave a little bow. Then he guided Tank off the dance floor to where Alan and George were getting ready to leave. Tank thanked the men for their help and paid his bill before heading out. Alan drove, and Tank settled in the back next to Collin, who yawned and leaned against him. Before Tank realized what had happened, Collin slipped his hand around Tank's waist and fell asleep.

"How can anyone be out that fast?" Tank whispered.

"Travel, hard work, and dancing will take a lot out of a fellow," George said, yawning himself.

Alan pulled to a stop at an intersection and looked back, shaking his head. "He was in the RAF for a few years, and those boys learn to sleep when they can."

"He flew planes?" Tank asked.

"Yes," George said. "Collin was danged good, from what I hear. But he had some vision issues, and they clipped his wings. After that, he went to work on the family estate, and things have been tough since then. He and the earl don't get along much. Not that anyone does with that man. Collin's father is barely tolerated, but he stays just over the line so that cutting him will cause talk and raise questions, so folks put up with the bastard, and he goes on being a pain in the bum."

Tank nodded. He hadn't pegged Collin as a military man, but then he was a pilot, so that was different. "I know he's good with horses."

"Collin is amazing with them. But his first love is flying. It always was," George said softly.

Tank hummed to himself. He thought that a guy like Collin would have had everything in life he could have wanted. His family had money and were well known. They had a title. But it seemed that he and Collin did have something in common. "I don't know what to say."

George turned in the passenger seat. "Just because I'm a duke and Collin is a viscount doesn't mean that we haven't had our share of disappointments just like everyone else. His life may not mirror yours, but it doesn't mean that he's had it easy. Just a different brand of hard road, and there's plenty of potholes ahead." George turned back around, and Tank held Collin to him for the rest of the drive back to the ranch.

A LITTLE while later, Collin sat up and rubbed his eyes. "Where are we? Is this the ranch?" He peered out the window.

"No. Alan got a call from Chip that some of the fence might be down. Alan is taking a look. He'll be back in a few minutes." Tank was so tempted to lean down and guide Collin's lips to his. They were alone in the car at the moment, and Collin's scent filled the confined space. It had been a very long time since he had been with anyone, and the desire that welled from deep inside was almost more than he could control, but Tank had to. There was no other choice. "Did you get a good rest?" He cracked the door open to let in some fresh air and hopefully cool some of the want that raged through him.

"You didn't help them?" Collin asked.

"Alan said he and George had it, and you were asleep." The front door opened and Alan got behind the wheel once again. "Is everything okay?"

"There was a small break, but we got it repaired, so nothing is going to get out in the night. I'll have one of the men come by in the morning to make a permanent repair." George got in as well, and Tank closed his door before they slipped off into the night back toward home.

Collin sat up and leaned back in the seat. Tank missed his warmth and closeness, but he didn't say anything about it. The few minutes he'd had Collin next to him had been special, but he didn't want to seem desperate. Once Alan turned in the drive and parked the car, Tank got out to a cry from the pups inside the house. The barking echoed out through the open windows.

"Sheba, that's enough," he called. As soon as he opened the door, all three of them raced outside around his legs, tails wagging. Collin lifted one of the puppies, giving it attention, while Tank got the others inside. He waved as George and Alan pulled out, and then closed the door before setting out to get the troops a little snack.

"I had a nice evening," Collin said as they watched the dogs eat. It was strange how neither of them seemed to want to part, and yet they didn't know what to say to each other. Tank found himself glancing at Collin, who seemed to do the same, and yet no words would come. He wasn't sure what to do and figured the best thing was to just go to bed.

The dogs finished eating, and Tank took all of them outside to do their business. When he returned, Collin seemed to have gone to bed, and Tank took the dogs with him to his room. After cleaning up, he climbed into a bed that seemed much bigger than it had before, and the house lonelier than he had ever realized. Tired and with a busy day ahead, he quickly fell asleep.

SOMETHING WAS off, but Tank couldn't quite figure out what. The house was quiet, with no unusual sounds. He sat up and checked the dogs but found their bed empty, which was unusual. He pushed back the covers and pulled on a pair of sweats. Then he quietly went through the house. A lone figure sat in front of the picture window in the living room, the dogs clustered around him. Collin petted all of them slowly and in turn. There was something about a man who cared for his dogs.

"Is something wrong?" Tank asked. "It's after three and you should be exhausted after all the work today."

"I know, but it's well past ten at home, and my body thinks I should be awake," Collin said. "I didn't mean to get you up. I just couldn't sleep." He turned in the chair, and the dogs huffed and whined until he settled and began petting them once more. Sheba jumped down, and Tank sat on the sofa and let her jump into his lap. "You should go back to bed. I know you have work you need to do in the morning, and I can help."

"I'm awake now, and I have to get up in about an hour anyway." Besides, in the light of the full moon that shone through the window, Collin looked like some ethereal god he'd had to read about in high school. Collin wore just a pair of shorts, and his light skin seemed to glow. He was slim but not skinny, and contrary to what Tank originally thought, Collin hadn't been some spoiled rich kid who spent his life taking it easy. There was work built up in those long, lean muscles. His hair caught the light like morning over a mown field of straw. "I can get us something to drink."

"It isn't necessary. I was hoping to try to rest again," Collin said. The two puppies curled together on his lap. "These guys are so cute."

"Chip rescued them, the way he does most living creatures. He has a whole passel of them at the ranch. Last year he had an eagle for a while. He found it injured back near the creek, and it couldn't fly. Got the vet to tranquilize it and splint the wing, and Chip nursed it back to health and set it free a month later. Now there's a nest back there, and maybe we'll get eaglets this year. That boy takes care of everything that crosses his path."

"Is he going to be a vet?"

"I sure hope so. The critters all trust him, and he seems to know what they need," Tank explained as his eyes began to grow heavy. He'd probably had more beer than he intended, and the residual was making him sleepy. "I think I'm going to try to go back to bed." Tank moved, and Sheba jumped down. Collin lifted the sleepy pups and set them down. They followed their mother down the hall, and Tank went to his room, then turned to where Collin stood outside his door. He met his gaze, and Collin slowly approached.

Tank stood stock-still as Collin came up to him. Collin took his hand and led him into the bedroom and to the bed. Tank thought about asking what they were going to do, but he didn't want to sound stupid. This was a man who understood the ways of the wide world. Tank knew his ranch, and that *was* his world. Collin climbed under the covers, and Tank slid off the sweatpants and got in too. "Just rest, okay?" Collin whispered, and when Tank lay against the pillow, Collin curled into his side, a hand sliding over his belly but going no farther. "Just relax and close your eyes. You feel like you're about to jump out of your skin."

Tank swallowed hard. "I don't want to mess anything up."

Collin patted his belly and shifted closer. "Just close your eyes and go to sleep. We can talk about anything more in the morning."

"But…," Tank said, his blood pumping a mile a minute.

"Hey," Collin whispered, using that same tone he had with the horse a day earlier. "There's nothing to worry about. I don't think you're ready for anything more than just a little quiet time." He yawned. "Relax and don't worry about anything."

"But you're in my bed." This was the most confusing thing Tank could remember. He hadn't had anyone in his bed in years, and that had most definitely been for sex, though Tank had thought it would mean more than that. He had been mistaken then, and now the rules seemed to have shifted once more.

Collin chuckled. "I can go back to my own bed if that's what you'd prefer."

He held Tank a little closer, and Tank figured what the hell. He could go with the flow. He didn't have to control everything all the time. He closed his eyes, breathed in Collin's scent, and tried to do as Collin said and let go of his issues, at least for now.

Collin rested his head on Tank's shoulder and seemed to settle on the bed. Tank tried not to stare up at the ceiling in wonder and confusion. He closed his eyes, breathed deeply, and let the day's work catch up with him.

TANK STARTLED awake as light streamed into his room. He blinked and checked the time. It was after seven, and Collin was asleep right next to him. He didn't want to move, but he had intended to get up two hours ago. There were chores to do and plenty of work to oversee, yet all that fell to the side with Collin next to him.

"Is it work time?" Collin asked with a yawn.

"I suppose it is." He left the covers in place. "There's a lot to get done."

"Then why aren't you moving?"

Tank was just about to say that he didn't want to when Sheba began barking, racing out the door with the puppies behind her, all three raising one hell of a ruckus. Tank pushed back the covers and got out of the bed, feeling Collin's eyes on him. He pulled on a pair of sweats and a T-shirt before heading to the door. He peered out the window at a truck he wasn't familiar with and wondered who could be here. "Calm down, beasts," he told the dogs, and opened the door.

CHAPTER 5

"WHAT ARE you doing here?" It wasn't the words but the tone that worried him. Collin got out of bed and hurried to his room, where he pulled on clothes before joining Tank in the living room. There, Tank was engaged in a staring contest with a rough-looking man with stone-cold eyes and a scraggly beard.

"You seem to be doing pretty well for yourself," the man said as Collin strode in. "You were always talking about this place, and I was in the area, so I thought I'd stop in to see my old Army buddy." There was something off in the way he spoke. His tone was soft but his expression hard.

"I see. Well, you've seen the place, and now it's time for you to move on." Tank was strung as tightly as the strings on the violin Collin's mother had forced him to learn to play. Sheba growled, and Tank lifted her up while Collin gathered the two puppies and took them to the chair.

"Who's your friend?" The man's gaze shifted to him, and Collin wished he'd stayed in the bedroom. The desire, almost lust, in his eyes made Collin want to shiver, but he refused to. Then the man turned to Tank, and the desire only grew.

So that was it.

"What do you want, Sullivan?" Tank asked. "I have work to do."

"Come on, Timmy. It's me." The tone changed completely, and his gaze softened. The guy seemed to be trying to catch Tank's interest. Too bad he didn't have anything to use as bait. It looked desperate and ridiculous. Collin could tell that at one point Sullivan had probably been a handsome man, with his cut cheekbones and huge eyes. His no-longer-regal nose had probably been broken more than once, the dark circles under his eyes told of a hard life, and his sallow skin said that Sullivan hadn't been eating well lately.

When Tank hesitated, Collin stood. "We need to feed the horses and check on the cattle," Collin offered.

Tank turned to him and seemed to snap back into himself. "Yes. I have a lot of work to do. It was good of you to visit and all, but this isn't a good time."

Sullivan put a hand on Tank's shoulder. His smile might have been stunning if his teeth weren't yellowed from tobacco. This was someone who had become accustomed to getting what he wanted from his looks and hadn't come to terms with the fact that they were gone. "I have a room in town for a few days. Maybe we can get together, like old times." He patted Tank's shoulder and then removed his hand. "You go ahead and do your ranch stuff. I'll be seeing you around." He turned and left the house, glancing back for a few seconds at Tank standing in the doorway before getting into an old blue truck and pulling out of the drive.

Tank finally closed the door, holding Sheba in front of him like she was a shield.

"Do I want to ask?"

Tank stood still, blinking like he was in shock. "I don't really want to talk about it."

"We all have a past, Tank." Collin held his gaze. "I went to a private school because it was expected. It was all boys, which worked out well for me because I wasn't interested in girls and didn't know what to do with them. But I had a crush on one of the other boys, and I couldn't say anything… until I accidentally did when I was in year ten. That was pretty awful, and he—well, I was so convinced he liked me back, and he told me he did, but all he was interested in were weekends at the estate and getting the opportunity to ride our horses." Collin refused to let himself blush. It had been years ago.

"I guess things ended badly," Tank said, letting Sheba get down.

Collin rolled his eyes. "He dumped me for someone else. It's the usual thing. But he asked if we could still be friends and then wondered if maybe he could come over the next weekend."

Tank's mouth hung open. "He was just interested in you for what you had."

"Yes. I learned quickly that the boys thought because I already had a title that I had a lot of money… and that apparently I was stupid and gullible. And maybe I am, because he was only the first." Collin sat down. "I have a history of picking the wrong guys." He met Tank's gaze, watching as he turned toward the door. "Maybe you do too?"

Tank shook his head. "Sullivan…. No, he and I were never like that."

That was a bit of a surprise. "But the whole Timmy thing and the way he was so touchy-feely?" Maybe that was how Americans behaved, but Collin didn't think so. "He sure tried to turn on the charm and everything, like he was trying to play on something."

"He was," Tank said. "Sullivan is always working an angle."

Collin rolled his eyes. "Maybe the man should try working a shower and making his way to a barber. He could use some help."

Tank set Sheba down. "That's exactly what he wants. Sullivan wants me to help him, but unfortunately, with Sullivan, no good deed goes unpunished."

"So this guy is flirting with you because he thinks you'll respond, since every gay man is out for any piece of arse he can get?" Collin was floored. "That guy is a sicko, if you ask me." That was an interesting idea, though just looking at the man was enough to make Collin's bollocks play hide-and-seek.

Tank shrugged. "I got to get to work." He tromped back down the hall, and the door to his room closed hard enough that Collin and the dogs jumped at the bang. Collin glanced down at Sheba, who looked back up at him in doggie confusion. Knowing there was nothing he could do, Collin went to his room, and the dogs followed.

Collin sat on the side of the bed, wondering what he had gotten himself into. He'd come all this way to spend some time on a ranch and get away from the mess at home. What he had been hoping for was to hit the love lottery like George had and find a guy like Alan. Instead, other than a guy at a bar, the only man he'd met was a cantankerous rancher who didn't seem to want to talk about anything. Granted, the man was as hot as Spain in July, but that was only going to get him so far. "What do you think, guys?" he asked Sheba and the pups, who had made themselves at home, curled up next to his holdall. They looked at him like he was crazy. Hell, maybe he was and he should have just stayed at home and endured his father's pain-in-the-bum remarks and attitude. It was probably stupid to think that lightning would strike for him, probably because he had been hoping for it.

The dogs were comfortable, and he hated to disturb them, so he dressed, then opened the door and left the room, noticing that the door to Tank's was still closed. He checked his phone—there was a message that breakfast was in an hour. With nothing else to do, he went to the barn, found a barrow, and figured there were always stalls to muck out. Maybe the physical exertion would help him work away some of this anxiety.

"WHAT ARE you doing?" Tank demanded in his deep, gruff voice that sent a thrill up Collin's spine.

"What does it look like?" Collin spread a load of bedding on the floor of the now-cleaned stall. "This was a real mess."

"What did you do with the horse that was in here?" Collin didn't understand his wide-eyed, panicked look.

"You mean Barney?" There had been no name tag, so Collin had just named him that in his head. He hadn't meant to say it out loud. "I put him in the stall over there for the moment. He was a little skittish at first, but then he wanted a scratch and I knew I'd won him over. The poor guy needs grooming, so I thought I'd do that before I put him back in his stall." Tank's eyes grew wide as dinner plates. "What?"

"That horse is messed up," Tank said. "He doesn't let me or anyone get close to him, except Chip. I have to ask him to come over so I can get him in from the pasture."

"What happened to him?" Collin asked softly, approaching the stall where the chestnut stallion looked over the wall with wild eyes. "It's okay, boy. No one is going to hurt you." Barney snorted and then calmed, bouncing his head. Collin gently petted his neck and gave him a carrot as a treat. "I know. You're completely misunderstood."

"Well I'll be damned," Tank muttered.

"Give us some distance. Breakfast is in a few minutes, and I'd like to brush him before I put him back. I'll meet you in the house." Collin didn't look away from Barney, keeping his tone gentle.

Tank whirled in his boots and left the barn, pulling the door closed behind him.

"You know, I think Tank is a lot of bluster." He thought he might have heard the barn door open once more. "I know he's big and looks kind of scary." Collin stroked Barney's nose before leaving to get the combs from the tack room.

He carefully opened the stall door, keeping his nerves tamped down deep. He stepped inside and gently closed the door before running his hand down Barney's back. The horse skittered a little, turning to look at him. "I'm just going to brush you, and you'll feel so much better.

I promise." His coat was ragged, and as Collin brushed him, Barney's undercoat came out on the brush. Barney made a shivery movement a number of times, and Collin knew it was his body trying to get rid of more of it. "I told you you'd like it." He worked quickly and efficiently, getting the horse brushed and cleaned. "Now you should see yourself." He really was a beautiful horse. Collin wondered who had done a number on him to make a gorgeous horse like this act so scared.

Collin finished and led Barney back to his stall, then closed the door quietly behind him. Then he put away the tools, figuring he'd clean out the stall that was now covered with hair after breakfast. He was starving.

Once he closed the barn door behind him, Tank stalked across the yard to meet him. "You know, that was a real dumb thing to do. That horse could have hurt you."

"I'm fine, and so is Barney. He's groomed and looks beautiful. I can see why you keep him." Collin refused to rise to Tank's worry. "I know my way around horses, and he just needs to learn to trust again. Where did you get him?"

"He's one of Chip's rescues," Tank said. "Just like Sheba and the pups. He was in terrible shape when Chip called me from the vet office. He had been on a call with Doc Stevenson and came across Barney, as you call him. He was emaciated and could barely stand. Doc called the sheriff, and they found a judge who ordered all the animals taken away. The place was wretched, according to Chip, and he needed a place for Barney. Their barn was full, so Chip brought him here. I think because Chip rescued him, Barney bonded with him. Anyone else he'll kick and bite. I got a scar from that damned horse's teeth," he snarled. "You and me need to get to breakfast, or else Maureen is going to send out the troops."

Collin hurried inside to wash his hands and then joined Tank at the truck. The man drove like a bat out of hell, and they arrived just as everyone was sitting down. "I was starting to think my breakfast wasn't good enough for you," Maureen teased as Collin loaded his plate with food.

"This is amazing." He dug right in the way the others did. Tank sat across from him, and Chip sat next to him on the bench seat nearest the windows. "I brushed Barney this morning."

Chip looked at Tank.

"That wild horse you talked me into," Tank clarified.

"He let you brush him?" Chip asked. "Good job."

"Damned horse won't let anyone get close," Tank muttered. "Don't know what I'm going to do with him."

Chip let Tank's grumpiness wash over his back and away. "He's a good horse. Old Man Carruthers let everything go, and that horse was just about gone. Instead, you got yourself a stallion with a great bloodline, just as soon as the judge signs off on turning him over to you permanently."

"But I can't get near him."

Chip chuckled. "But Collin can, so let him work with Barney." He smiled. "Where did that name come from?"

"He needed one, so that's what I called him," Collin said with a grin. "He looked like a Barney to me. Anyway, he let me brush him, and I had no trouble moving him through the barn." He turned to Tank. "Maybe I can work with him. Get him to calm down a little and used to people again." He set down his fork. "If someone treated me that badly, I'd be snarly too." He wanted to ask Tank what his excuse was, but he lowered his gaze from the huge man's and went back to his breakfast.

"Did you sleep well at Tank's?" Maureen asked. It was an innocent question, but Collin smirked as Tank squirmed in his chair.

"I slept great, and I think Tank did too, because he wasn't up as early." He held Tank's gaze, liking the fact that the huge man seemed nervous and jumpy. Collin had no intention of saying anything about spending part of the night in Tank's bed, but he liked that the idea of it getting out seemed to unnerve Tank. The guy needed to be shaken up a little.

"I heard about the two of you last night," Maureen said. "Wish I'd been there to see you dancing." The lady had a wicked sense of humor and was definitely trying to get under Tank's skin.

"Teddy is still shaking in his boots, I bet," Chip said, adding his own two cents, and Tank nearly dropped his fork.

"That's enough," Alan said. "Tank is a guest in this house, and you all need to stop."

Collin lowered his gaze, Chip colored a little, and even Maureen seemed ashamed. "Sorry, Tank," Chip said softly. "But it was pretty cool, especially the way you charged in there. Like you were rescuing Collin from the sharks. Though Teddy Welder is more like a minnow."

"Chip," Alan said with a warning in his voice, and Chip sighed.

"Tank is a good dancer, though," Chip went on, ignoring Alan. "Isn't he, Collin?"

Collin lifted his gaze to Tank's. "He most definitely is." And there was one thing he knew: a good dancer on the floor meant rhythm in other places too. "And Alan is right. I don't think Tank likes being the topic of discussion." He snagged another pancake. "What's the project for the day?"

"I already mended that section of fence and have some men out riding the rest to check for more weak spots." Alan seemed to have slipped into being in charge, even though Collin was under the impression his mother ran the ranch. "What else is on your list?"

"Everyone has their assignments already, and Chip is working a shift at the clinic." She gave her youngest son a look, and Chip finished eating and hurried off and out of the house. "That boy loves God's creatures, but he never met a clock he could read."

Collin finished eating and looked around the table. There had to be something he could do. "Tank, what about the barn? There was plenty I could do there."

Tank nodded and set his napkin on the table next to his empty plate. "Thank you, Maureen. A great breakfast as usual. I got plenty to do." He pushed back his chair, and Collin said his own thank-yous and followed Tank outside. "You don't need to come with me. Maybe you can stay here and spend some time with your friends." He was already striding toward the truck.

"So you don't need help, then?" Collin called back, hands on his hips, glaring at Tank's back.

Tank paused outside the truck, hand on the handle, and Collin figured Tank was going to leave without him. He had a sharp retort about Tank running away on the tip of his tongue, but he turned.

"A rancher always needs help," Tank said, and Collin strode to the truck and climbed inside. The house's front window curtains slid back into place as Tank backed the truck out into the drive.

ALAN STOOD next to George in the living room. "A twenty says that they end up punching each other before the trip's over."

George bumped Alan's hip. "You're on. If it's a shag-or-brawl situation, I say they end up shagging each other's brains out before too long."

"You know, with cowboys, those two things aren't mutually exclusive." Alan chuckled as he stepped away from the window, sliding his arm around George's waist.

CHAPTER 6

AS SOON as he parked the truck, Tank got out and stalked up to the house. He hated being picked on and made fun of. That had happened all his damned life, and he wasn't going to stand for it now.

Inside, he fed the dogs, grateful that Collin had the good sense to stay the hell away. He wasn't angry with him, or even Chip, but at the world, and he needed a chance to come to grips with things. Collin hadn't known how Tank felt, nor did any of the guys. But inside, he was as riled and twisted as a bale of barbed wire.

No matter what he felt, Tank had been trained to bury it down deep and to think. Be logical and don't lose your head. That was how to stay alive in battle, and he had taken that lesson to heart.

He stood at the sink and listened to the dogs as they ate, Sheba's tag ringing against the stainless-steel bowl. He needed to calm down. The guys hadn't meant anything by what they said. In fact, he knew that their picking on him was a sign of affection. These were his friends, and he would do anything for Maureen and her family, but it was difficult when old hurts—memories and pain that had nothing to do with them—got activated.

A high-pitched whinny caught his ear through the open window. Sheba barked, and Tank headed for the back door and raced out across the yard.

"That's it. You're okay," Collin said as he let the lead go slack. Barney stood, muscles tense, as Collin clicked his tongue.

Tank held his breath, hoping to hell the horse didn't decide to run Collin down, but he began walking. Collin kept the lead loose and let him go in a slow circle. "You're pretty amazing, you know that?" Collin said just loudly enough for Tank to hear the words on the breeze. Barney turned his ears, straining to listen as he picked up speed.

"Don't go too fast," Tank said.

Collin nodded to let him know he'd gotten the message. "You just need some exercise, don't you, boy?" He turned as Barney continued trotting around the ring. "That's what's got you all pent up. You have all this energy and no way to let it out." Collin kept him moving for a good half hour and then slowed him to a walk to let the horse cool off before gently leading him back into the barn.

"Are you crazy?" Tank asked Collin as soon as he stepped outside once more. "That horse could have taken your arm off or decided he was going to run away with you."

Collin stared at him like *he* was crazy. "I would have dropped the lead. He's been on one before and knew what to do. I think the guy is just out of his head with fear, and doing something familiar could help him get past his issues." He put his hands on his hips. "I know this is your ranch, but I also know horses. I've worked with them my entire life." The heat in Collin's eyes was attractive, but Tank forced himself to take a step back.

"Then you should have known to take it easy with him."

"I did. I didn't try to mount or saddle him. All we did was work in the ring, and he settled down after a while and seems calmer now." Collin stepped closer. "Are you angry because you think I don't know what I'm doing or because this is your ranch and you want to be the one calling all the shots? Maybe I should have asked you, but I'm confident in my abilities, and I thought I could help Barney—and you as well, because if he becomes more comfortable in his own skin, then he might be useful for breeding."

Tank took a deep breath and tried to calm himself. As soon as he'd stepped outside and seen Collin with Barney, the top of his head had nearly blown off. All he could see was Barney hurting Collin or trampling him in a panic. "We need to talk about things before you do them. This is my ranch, and I'm responsible for everything that happens here." He hoped Collin could understand that.

"I was only trying to help," Collin said.

"I know that, and you may have, but...." Tank closed his mouth. "Let's just talk about things before we do them, okay?"

Collin nodded. "All right." He sighed. "I guess I'm used to doing what I want with the horses. My father doesn't get out there with them any longer. He leaves that to me and his turf manager."

Tank could understand that Collin was used to making his own decisions. This was Tank's place, but he wasn't going to say that. Collin had had good intentions, and Tank couldn't argue that Barney would be valuable for the ranch if he did calm down.

"So what's up next, oh fearless leader?" Collin asked, and Tank would have rolled his eyes, but when Collin headed to the barn, he got a good look at him in those damned tight jeans. The mental list that Tank worked from suddenly blanked on him, and all he could do was stare. "Are you going to look at my bum all day, or are we going to get to work?" Collin continued toward the barn, and Tank groaned, pushing down the fantasies that sprang to life like spring daisies.

TANK'S SHIRT clung to his skin. He pulled it away to get a little air, but it vacuum-sealed itself right back into place within seconds. "How come you aren't soaked through?" he asked, looking Collin over as he closed the stall door. The barn smelled fresh and clean, which was how Tank liked it.

Collin cocked his nose a little higher. "I'm an aristocrat, and we never sweat." He glared as if offended for about two seconds before smiling. "Actually I have no idea, other than the fact that I'm not a walking wall of muscle." His eyes grew heated, and Tank set the shovel aside as Collin drew closer.

A noise at the door distracted Tank from the intensity of Collin's eyes. "Isn't this a pretty sight," Sullivan drawled.

Tank stilled and turned toward the door. "This is my barn on my land, and you don't get to make your slurs or dirty insinuations here." Sullivan's stance shifted immediately. "I suggest you leave now. You showed up looking for something you aren't going to find here... or anywhere else."

"Really?" He pushed away from the doorframe. "I think you and I need to have a little talk alone." He tilted his head outside.

Tank turned away and took care of the tools. Then he put the wheelbarrows back where they belonged before returning to where Collin waited, looking between the two of them like he was watching some silent tennis match.

Finally Tank stepped out of the barn. "I'll ask one last time before I kick your ass off my property. What do you want?"

"I'm broke and I need help."

Tank leaned closer. "More like you have no money and you need a fix." Oh, he knew that hollow look in Sullivan's eyes and what the sallow color meant. "There were rumors you were on shit years ago, and it looks like your choices are catching up with you."

Sullivan poked him in the chest. "Don't you talk to me about choices, like when you turned and ran, leaving me to take the flak." He glared, those eyes as cold as December wind.

"You can remember things any way you want. But we were told to pull back, and you ignored it. That isn't my fault or anyone else's." Tank let his gaze grow as hard as Sullivan's.

"Oh yeah? Well, I was the one who got injured because you and Westerhouse ran like little girls, and I can prove it. Pull back or not, you aren't supposed to leave your buddy behind." He sneered.

Tank rolled his eyes. "You were never my buddy. All you did was cajole and try to get whatever you could from anyone and everyone. You were a thief, and I can prove that," Tank said. "So whatever you got planned, you need to think twice." Sullivan stiffened, and Tank knew he was gearing up for a fight. "Get off my land and get out of town."

Collin appeared next to him. "I know the likes of you," he said in a deep, rich accent that made him sound like the king himself. "Tank asked you to leave, and I suggest you go."

"And who the fuck are you?" Sullivan snapped.

Collin stood tall, hat on his head, gaze as tough as nails. Fuck, it was exciting to see Collin worked up and yet as calm and cool as a glass of iced tea. "The Viscount Haferton and the future Earl of Doddington. The real question is, what kind of dirt are you? I may not be from this area, but I know you don't threaten a man on his own land and expect to get away with it. Now, whatever you seem to think Tank has done, that's in the past. I suggest you put this little visit of yours in the past as well and move on."

Sullivan leaned forward. "You don't know the first thing about the man you're defending."

"I know enough about him… and about you." His lips drew into a line, and those eyes blazed with anger. "No matter what Tank might have done, you don't have the right to try to use anything to your advantage here. That just makes you a snake, and we chop the heads off those when we find them around the horses."

Sullivan paled. "You haven't heard the last of this."

Collin laughed. "What a git. You sound like a bad TV villain. Try to come up with something original next time. Now go to that piece of shite you call a truck and get out of here." Collin's hands went to his hips, and Tank already figured that when Collin did that, he was dug in and ready for battle.

"Got to have some fancy-pants fight your battles for you?" Sullivan spat.

"No. He can beat the piss out of you. I'm just here as backup and to take out the rubbish when it's over." Damn, Collin had a tongue as sharp as one of Maureen's butcher knives. He actually followed Sullivan to his truck, glaring until Sullivan turned out of the drive. Then he whirled around and clomped back to where Tank stood completely stunned. "What the hell is it with him? He thinks of himself as some supervillain."

"Maybe because he's twisted and all kinds of messed up." Tank didn't know what else to say. "I'm assuming you heard everything."

Collin patted his shoulder. "I did, and Tank, everyone has a past they aren't happy with. That doesn't mean that a guy like that gets to use it to his advantage." He headed toward the house, and Tank couldn't help wondering if Collin would feel the same way if he knew the whole story.

"I need to check on the herd. You go on inside. I'll be back in a few hours." Tank strode over to one of the ATVs and jumped on to take off across the land.

THE HERD was fine. They had water and plenty of area to graze. But Tank had known that before he left.

Tank had spent the years since getting out of the service bringing his ranch back from the brink, and he'd done it himself. He was used to being on his own and liked it that way. Or at least he thought he had. Collin had been staying with him for a few days, and already Tank was getting used to having him around. And when Collin had stood beside him, not knowing anything about him, it touched something in Tank.

"What the hell is wrong with me?" he asked out loud as he stood on a rise, watching the cattle eat. There was something peaceful about this spot.

Of course he didn't get an answer. Maybe there wasn't one. Collin was going to be here for just a week and a half, and then he'd go back to England and Tank would be alone once more. Everything would go back to the way it was. The real trouble was that Tank wasn't sure that was what he wanted.

Knowing everything was all right with the herd, he jumped back on the ATV to return to the house.

Clouds built before he was halfway back, and thunder rolled over the land as the house came into sight. The first raindrops hit the dry ground as he pulled into the equipment shed and turned off the engine.

Whinnies carried on the wind, and Tank raced to the barn. Collin was leading one of the horses inside, and she was fighting him. Still, Collin got her in, and Tank went for the last one still out in the driving wind.

"That's it. It's okay," he told Rattler as he led him toward the barn. A crack of thunder split the air, and Rattler reared and bolted. Tank fell back and landed flat on the ground, rain pelting him as he stared up at a turbulent sky, unable to move as Rattler ran and jumped with each clap of thunder. Tank knew those hooves could land on him at any moment, and there wasn't a damned thing he could do about it.

"Tank!" Collin raced over. "Back off," he snapped at the horse, who moved away as Collin waved his arms. "Are you okay?" he asked. "Is anything broken?"

Tank shook his head, finally able to move. Collin helped him up, got him standing, and led Tank to the rail. Then Collin went for Rattler. He got him into the barn as Tank took his first steps and got himself out of the rain.

"Jesus," Tank said, able to breathe again.

"That storm came out of nowhere," Collin said as he closed the last stall door. "All the horses are inside, and I have them settled with some feed. Is that all there is to it?"

Tank turned, using one of the stall walls to prop himself up. The rain was already letting up, and the wind seemed to have passed as well. "Sometimes all we get is the lightning, with no rain at all." He breathed as deeply as he could, his head clearing and his hands no longer shaking. At least it continued raining and wasn't so hard that it couldn't soak into the ground where it was needed. Of course, once the sun came out, the humidity would go through the roof.

"Will the horses be okay here inside?" Collin asked.

"We can let them back out in their paddocks in a few minutes." A little rain wouldn't hurt them, and they could graze outside easy enough. "But keep Barney in here."

"He did fine during the storm," Collin said. "I think his issue is with people."

Tank could understand. "Sometimes I wonder if he and I have the same damned issue."

Collin opened the side doors to let in some air and then came over next to him.

"Thank you for helping me." He was okay now.

"You aren't sore?"

Tank shook his head. "Just got the wind knocked out of me."

"Good." Collin stepped closer and tugged at his collar, pulling Tank down and into a kiss that threatened to steal the breath he'd just caught.

"Hey, boss," one of the men called, and Collin backed away before heading toward the house. Tank blinked as Hatcher Belton strode over. "That section of fence you wanted checked is done." He pulled off his hat to reveal a patch of short black curls. "Everything is okay, but a tree came down. It spared the fence, but we need to get it out of the pasture. You want me and a few of the guys to take care of it?"

"Please," Tank said, wondering how the men who worked for him would react if they saw Collin kissing him. Knowing a guy liked bulls was one thing, but seeing it was another.

"Cool. We'll get 'er done." He smiled and turned away, then paused. "That fella staying with you, that viscount fella? I think he likes you." Tank growled. "I know, you don't like to talk about shit like that. But you're smiling." He tipped his hat and then hurried back to his truck and took off.

Tank strode to the house, where he found Collin sitting on the sofa, surrounded by the dogs. "Did I get you in trouble somehow?"

"How would you do that?" Tank asked. "I'm the boss, and all my guys know I'm gay. Hell, I danced with you in front of half the town. Do you think everyone within a hundred miles doesn't know that I like you?" He sat down next to him.

"Then why don't you do something about it?" Collin asked. "I like you too." He leaned against Tank's arm. "It took all my willpower not to jump you last night. But it didn't seem like you were ready for something like that."

Tank's heart beat faster, and he wasn't sure if Collin was going to kiss him or not. "I guess I have a terrible record with relationships."

Collin looked into his eyes. "We all do until we meet the person who is right for us. Do you think we all meet that one special person at university or just walking down the street when we're eighteen years old?" He shook his head. "You have to kiss a lot of frogs before you meet your prince. I've kissed plenty."

Tank snickered. "You kiss frogs? Don't they give you warts?"

"Smartarse," Collin retorted. "And no, I don't have warts. But I did date guys who just wanted me for my title. Then there was Howard, who thought he could ingratiate himself to the earl. That ended badly all around because I didn't want anything to do with anyone my father might like… and there is no sucking up to that prickly bastard anyway." He sighed and shifted on the sofa. "The one time I did really think I had met a special guy… well, he died. That was when I was at university."

Tank leaned closer, listening. "What happened?" he asked softly.

"Chester was a literature scholar. He sometimes had a hard time getting around and used a cane. He and I had a lecture together, and we spent a lot of time working together. That led to… well… maybe a romance of sorts. He was sweet and exceedingly kind. Smart too—really smart. He and I started dating. We had coffee and went to a few films. I really liked him. But then the term ended and we both went home. When I got back, I looked for him, but Chester never returned. I asked around the school, but no one knew what happened. I contacted his family in Surrey and found out that Chester had a heart condition, and he had spent much of the break in the hospital. So I found out where and went up to see him." Collin swallowed. When he spoke again, his voice broke. "He was so weak and told me that there wasn't much hope. His heart had had more than it could take." His eyes filled with tears. "He died a few days later." Collin shrugged. "I didn't even realize how I felt about him until he was gone."

"Then you kissed all the frogs," Tank said. "You were trying to find someone like Chester?"

"Maybe. But there is no one like him. He was special… and perfect, because he never got the chance to be anything else. But none of the guys I dated ever came close to measuring up because I chose the wrong kind of guys."

Tank leaned closer. "What's the right kind?" He held his gaze, and Collin gently stroked his cheek. He wondered if Collin thought he could be that kind of guy. What surprised him was that he *wanted* to be.

"I wish I knew. I always thought I would know him when I met him." Collin nodded as he smiled and closed the distance between them.

Tank kissed Collin softly, but Collin had other ideas, pressing harder against him, deepening the kiss and sending Tank on a heated journey that he hoped would never stop. "Do you think I'm the kind of person you've been looking for?" Damn, he'd spent most of his life keeping his thoughts and feelings to himself, and with a single kiss Collin had him running off at the mouth.

"I don't know. But maybe we can try to figure things out."

"I see," Tank said and pulled Collin into his arms to kiss him back. "This could be a really interesting puzzle for both of us."

Collin cupped his cheeks in warm hands. "Yes, it definitely could."

CHAPTER 7

COLLIN WASN'T sure what he was feeling. He'd never gone for men like Tank, and yet he couldn't stop thinking about him. Being wrapped in his strong arms was hot and sexy as hell. Collin slid his hands down Tank's impressive chest, returning the kiss, straddling Tank's lap, and hanging on as Tank held him tighter.

"Is this what you want?" Tank whispered.

"Hell yes!" He wasn't going in for any of this whispering. He was going to make sure Tank heard him loud and clear.

"But aren't you afraid of doing what you did before?" Clearly he'd been listening to Collin's story.

"Maybe a little." He had expected Tank to be a go-for-it kind of guy. Maybe it was his size, but the big guys he'd known had all been real take-charge kind of men, and Tank seemed more laid-back. Not that Collin thought it bad for a second.

Tank pulled away. "Then how do you expect to get something different if you do the same things over and over?"

Collin climbed down and sat back next to him. "If you're not really interested, then I can understand that, and…." He felt like an idiot for throwing himself at Tank. Like in the past, he'd kiss a guy and then be ready to go for it.

Tank gently cradled his chin. "I think you're wonderful, but I don't jump into most things quickly. I can't afford to. Every time I rush ahead, people get hurt…. I get hurt." He leaned forward, the kiss sweet and gentle. "I think you and I need to give things a chance and take a little time. I know that you're only here for a little more than a week, but rushing into things isn't something that I think we should do." Tank sat back on the sofa. "And you deserve something more than a quick fuck on the sofa."

And just like that, Collin realized that beneath the hard-looking exterior was a man with a gentle soul—and maybe that truly was the kind of person he'd been searching for all this time. Collin knew he had to find out.

"IS THERE a truck I can borrow?" Collin asked Alan at dinner that evening.

Alan smiled and shrugged. "There's one you can use, but do you think that's a good idea? You're used to driving on the left, and it's not as easy to switch as I thought it would be."

Collin smirked. Alan's tribulations with driving back home were legendary in the area. After that, George had given him specific driving lessons. "I know. But I was hoping to go somewhere interesting with Tank, and I want it to be a surprise." He wasn't even sure where to go.

"Okay, I know just the place," Alan said with a grin. "And I can get you a vehicle, but only if you let me take you out driving."

"What are you two up to?" George asked from the other side of the table.

"Nothing," Alan said, winking at George, who rolled his eyes. Thankfully, Tank seemed intent on his dinner and hadn't noticed any of the conversation. He'd been quiet the last few hours before dinner and spent time out in the yard, clearing asway the limbs the storm had brought down.

George leaned over the table after glancing at Tank. "Talk to one of his men and ask them to saddle Tank's horse. Instead of using a truck, go out riding. The man is a cowboy, and there's nothing as... stimulating... as a ride." He bumped Alan's shoulder, and Collin nodded, refusing to ask any more questions about the exact type of riding his friends had been doing. He really didn't want to go there, and certainly not at dinner.

"Thank you for that," Collin said, making Alan and George laugh and drawing the attention of the rest of the people at the table. Except Tank, who still seemed off in his own little world.

"Don't worry. It's supposed to be a nice evening. I can call over and ask Hatcher to have everything ready for when you get back. I also have the perfect place to ride out to. There's a great section of the stream that runs along our properties, and it's perfect for a late-evening ride under the moon." He winked again, and Collin nodded.

"Thanks."

"No problem." Alan pulled out his phone and sent a message.

"Alan," Maureen said when she realized what he was doing. "Not at my table."

Alan smirked. "It's a humanitarian mission," he remarked flatly, nodding to Collin before slipping his phone away once more. Maureen rolled her eyes and then shot Alan a glare that he pretended he hadn't seen. His phone tinged, and Alan snuck a look at it. "All set for an hour." He slipped his phone away again, and Collin nodded his thanks.

"WHERE ARE we going?" Tank asked a little more than an hour later as they headed out under the glow of a full moon. Collin had a flashlight that he used to shine the way ahead.

"To a place that Alan told me about." He was used to darkness out on the estate, but even with the moon, it was surprisingly dark out here. Still, Collin could make out the outline of Tank's form on the horse, as well as enough of the landscape to be safe. The stars overhead seemed near to the ground, and Collin stopped himself from trying to reach out and touch them. The illusion was so stunning and the night amazingly clear. "He said it was straight out from the house and that I had to turn left when we reached the trees near the creek." He was starting to think this was a bad idea. He didn't know the area and should have just told Tank what he had in mind rather than dragging them both out in the middle of the night.

"Don't worry. I know where we're going." He clicked his teeth, and the horses picked up speed. Collin moved with the rhythm of the horse, watching the area as well as Tank, whose silhouette against the sky was like a cowboy postcard. As big as he was, on horseback, his movements were nonetheless graceful.

Collin followed Tank until they reached the darkness of the trees. "It's okay," Tank said as he pulled to a stop and dismounted, then shone a small pen light while he tied up his horse. Then he held Collin's until he dismounted and lashed his horse's reins to the same tree.

"Alan said we should go this way," Collin said, and Tank led him through the trees until they passed into a clearing with a stream running through the middle of it. "This must be it."

"I'd think so," Tank said. "This is one of Alan's favorite places. He and I used to come here as kids."

Collin handed Tank the pack Alan had given him, and he spread out the blanket on the ground. "I take it you were friends." He sat down.

Tank walked toward the creek, the water gurgling over the rocks, filling the night with comfort. "Alan and I grew up together. Our fathers were friends for years. At Christmas, Maureen and my mom used to spend days together baking and getting ready for the holiday. My mother passed away years ago, and Dad just after I left the service. Alan's dad passed a few months later. But growing up, we all played in the stream during the summer. There's a swimming hole a little ways upstream, and we used to sneak away to get some relief from the heat."

"Did Alan bring George out here?"

Tank laughed. "I doubt it. They met in the winter. But Alan used to bring people out here when he was growing up. It was like our own private boys' club." He turned around and sat next to Collin, who lay back, looking up at the sky.

"Did you and Alan ever…?" He let the words hang in the air.

"No," Tank breathed. "He and Chip are like my brothers." He turned toward Collin. "And Maureen is closer to an aunt than a friend. After Mother died, she made sure that I had a female presence in my life." Tank's voice broke, and Collin took his hand but otherwise pretended not to notice. "My mother and father…."

Collin figured Tank would stop speaking at any moment. He rarely said much, and he'd talked a lot already. "You don't have to. I know being quiet is easier for you."

"I had a brother, Benny. He was twelve when he died. He contracted meningitis. They can say what they want, but Mom died of grief. I don't think my father ever got over it either. When we were kids, all four of us would come to the stream to swim." He rolled onto his side. "Honestly, it's been a long time since I was here."

Collin gently touched Tank's sun-weathered face. "I'm sorry." Grief and pain he could understand. He'd held enough of it inside for a long time. Maybe he and Tank were more alike than Collin thought. Tank grew quiet and withdrew from people. Collin had been taught to bury his feelings, keep a stiff upper lip, present a proper visage to the world. But in the end, the loss was the same… and so was the hurt.

"No. I think it's time I told someone," Tank said softly as the water continued its perpetual gurgling. Collin closed his eyes and let the sound wash over him.

Tank lay back, and Collin took his hand once more. "I had hoped to bring you out here to look at the stars and...."

"You were hoping for a little cowboy romance?" Tank said.

"Well, yeah. This is lovely right here. The stars, the water...." He sat up. "And you." He leaned over Tank and kissed him gently. "You're lovely too."

Tank laughed, full and loud. "I have been called many things. A surly bastard, frightening, a quiet asshole... you name it. The guys in my unit called me Tank, and it stuck. No one I can remember has ever called me lovely." He put his arms around Collin's neck and drew him closer.

"Well," Collin whispered, "even the surliest bastard should be lovely to someone." He swallowed hard as Tank's heated breath kissed his cheeks. The truth was that Tank was hot, pure banked fire hiding behind those eyes, and Collin knew that under all that control was a blaze just waiting to explode.

"Please...," Tank said, and Collin drew closer.

"I mean it. You are damned hot, and everyone sees it. The girls all watch you, and the gay men all want to be right where I am now." He could have pressed it, but he had learned his lesson. Whatever happened, Tank had to be the one to make the first move. Collin lay back once again, looking up at the stars.

Tank lay still, his breathing mixing with the sound of the breeze through the trees. Collin waited, and then Tank's hand slid into his. Collin squeezed it back, and that was enough.

"Did you ever look up at the stars back home?" Tank asked.

"Yes. Mom was a horsewoman through and through. She used to ride most days and loved to play polo. Before I was born, she told me she played with the men and kicked their bums. On clear evenings, we'd ride out like we did tonight and lie out on the great lawn of the estate." He pointed to the sky. "That's Cassiopeia. But I call her Violet, because after she died, I swore I could see another star up there. So I always think of that as Mom." He squeezed Tank's hand. "I know it sounds bonkers and that Mom isn't up in the stars, but it's nice thinking that she could be up there."

Tank didn't say anything for a minute, not that Collin expected him to. Then, "You know, Benny used to love fishing. There are trout in this stream, and he used to sneak away so he could try to catch one. Maybe he's up there too, casting his line and trying to catch Pisces."

Collin smiled. He liked that image. "I always wanted a brother." He squeezed Tank's hand, and they lay quietly for a while. Collin's mind wandered over the man next to him. "You know, when I met you, I thought you were some sort of cowboy stereotype—big, hunky, like the Marlboro man. But...." He didn't know quite what to think.

"I'm not. I don't think anyone is... or ever was... not really. People out west who make their living off the land... we're who we are. We have traditions and ways of doing things, but we're the same as you."

Collin smiled to himself. "No, you are not. You're straightforward and honest. You tell things the way they are. You don't accept or condone a bunch of bullshit. Back home, my life is nothing but social subterfuge, vying for influence, and social niceties that hide a knife in the back. Everyone in my social circle would think nothing of smiling at me and shaking my hand while in my own home, and as soon as I left the room, speaking badly about me because I'm gay or don't fit the mold they think I should."

"Is that why you came here?" Tank asked. He'd asked the question before, and Collin had struggled a little with the answer. But he knew more now about what he should expect and what he'd found. "Because you wanted to get away from the folks at home? Because running from stuff ain't no way to find what you want."

"No. I came here to try to find something, and at the time I thought I was looking for someone. But maybe what I'm searching for is more of an idea."

Tank turned his head. "You know, you ain't going to find anyone until you know who you are. You gotta start with this." He placed his hand in the center of Collin's chest. "It all starts here."

Tank was right. Collin had been searching for a type of guy, but maybe what he really needed was to figure out what he truly wanted.

AFTER AN hour talking quietly and looking at the stars, he and Tank rode back to the ranch, guided by the lights outside the horse barn. Once they had the horses settled, Collin walked inside with Tank, just as curious about what the big man wanted as he was when they'd left on their ride. The dogs were happy as all heck when they returned, jumping over each other for attention. Collin played with them while Tank gave them each a treat.

"You want a beer?" Tank asked, handing Collin a can. "I don't have anything really nice, but I can look to get some tomorrow."

Collin looked it over. He was used to drinking his beer at the proper temperature but said nothing, instead opening the can. As soon as he took a taste, he was grateful for the chill to take the edge off the sharpness.

"Is it that different?"

"It is." Actually the stuff tasted awful, but he drank it anyway, sitting at Tank's scarred kitchen table. "What do we have to do for tomorrow?"

"We need to help Alan and Maureen. One of the barns they use to store winter feed needs to be rebuilt. It's in bad shape. Alan thinks we can get the old one down tomorrow. He has the supplies to start building a new one. Apparently all the neighbors are heading over to get the shell raised."

"I've heard about these barn raisings...." He'd actually thought it was more of a legend than a real occurrence. "I can help if you think there will be things I can do." He lowered his gaze. "I've done a few DIY projects."

"It's a big job, and there will be maybe thirty or forty men. It's a pretty simple building, and Alan messaged that the foundation and anchors are good. So we tear down what's there and take it apart. Then we rebuild something along the same lines."

"Okay." Collin finished the beer and yawned. "I should go to bed." He took care of his empty can and leaned down to kiss Tank good night before heading down the hall to his room.

While Collin cleaned up, he could hear Tank moving around the house. Then he climbed between the crisp sheets, thinking about Tank in the next room, trying to keep his imagination from running wild. There was something about him. The more he learned about Tank, the more curious he became, especially when it came to Sullivan, who seemed to think he had some leverage over him.

COLLIN TRIED to sleep. He knew he needed to, but his mind kept churning things over. His father and what he wanted, thoughts of Tank. Even his mother played a role in his nocturnal musings. The thing was, he wasn't sure what to do about any of it. Collin was fairly certain that his father was not going to let him just leave for two weeks without exacting some sort of price. That was the way the old asshole worked.

Talking to Tank brought back memories of his mother, and he played over the times they'd spent together. It had been she who had first taken him to London and shown him the National Gallery, the British Museum, and so many more things. She had even taken him to his first West End show and the ballet and opera.

Then there was Tank. Collin didn't quite know what to make of him, but he hoped he'd have the chance to figure it out.

He checked the clock next to the bed and pushed back the covers, then got up and went out to the living room to sit on the sofa. Sheba must have heard him, because she came out and jumped onto the sofa before curling up on his lap. Maybe it was still the time difference and he just wasn't used to it yet. Collin wasn't sure. Picking up the remote, he turned on the telly, made sure the volume was low, and settled in to watch *Lucifer*. He had seen some of the episodes back home, and the station seemed to be running a marathon of some sort, so he got comfortable and hoped something to take his mind off his circular thoughts would help him sleep.

"Are you still not tired?" Tank asked in a sleep-roughened voice.

"Sorry. I didn't mean to wake you," Collin said, turning to look. He about swallowed his teeth. Tank wore just a pair of boxers, and damn, Collin's imagination had not done the man justice. Tank was big all over, with strong arms, and a chest and belly covered with a light pelt of short hair that tapered down his belly before disappearing into his waistband. Maybe Collin was more tired than he thought, because he couldn't stop his gaze from following the trail. And *big all over* was exactly right.

"It was Sheba. She decided to make a production of walking over me before leaving the bed." Tank yawned and rubbed the center of his chest.

"I see." Maybe he should send her a thank-you bag of dog treats. "I don't know why I can't sleep. I should be able to after all the activity today." He shifted on the sofa, trying to hide the fact that Tank standing there wearing so damned little, those shorts hanging on his hips, was raising a great deal of interest. "It's also well into the morning back home, and my body could be a little confused still." There was a seven-hour time difference.

Collin squirmed under Tank's gaze, but Tank made no further move, so Collin figured he might as well go back to bed and try to sleep. Fatigue was catching up with him, and all those swirling thoughts from earlier had taken wing as soon as Tank walked into the living room.

"I'll see you in the morning." He gently lifted Sheba and then stood, passing her to Tank, who cradled the small dog to his ample chest. No matter what Tank did, he looked hotter and sexier by the second. Collin huffed softly to himself and went into his room, reminding himself that no one died from a case of blue bollocks, but he swore he was going to put that theory to the test soon enough. Maybe tomorrow he'd think about going back to that bar and seeing if Teddy was there. The thought put a smirk on his lips as he closed his eyes, until footsteps approached the door.

CHAPTER 8

COLLIN'S EYES were closed when Tank peered into the room. One thing he hated was indecision. On the battlefield, that could get your unit wiped out faster than making the wrong decision because it paralyzed everyone, and that was exactly how Tank felt: completely paralyzed. He just stood there, looking at Collin's sleek form outlined under the sheet. Sheba had trotted off as soon as he put her down, so he was truly alone, not that his dog had the answers he needed.

"Tank," Collin said softly, his voice entreating and gentle, but otherwise there was no movement. He didn't lift the covers in silent invitation or even crook his elegant finger in his direction. Nothing at all. Tank had no doubt that Collin was interested. His kisses and actions had told Tank Collin wanted him, and he wanted Collin. But Tank was torn. If he did this and gave in, then it was the same as admitting that his heart wanted Collin, and what the hell did he do in less than two weeks when Collin went home? Tank would be alone again. He could take that, but it would be worse knowing what it felt like have someone there.

God, sometimes he wondered if his childhood bullies had been right and he really did act like a girl. Not that there was anything wrong with girls, but those taunts stuck in the back of his mind.

"What are you doing?" Collin asked.

"I don't know," Tank answered even as Collin's rough voice called him. His feet took those first steps without Tank really thinking about it. He simply moved forward, and once he did, Collin pulled back the covers. Tank lay down, and Collin stayed on the other side of the bed.

"Do you know what you want?" Sometimes the simplest sentiment could mean so much. In that second Tank knew.

"Yes," Tank answered, snapping out of his haze and rolling onto his side. He drew Collin to him, bringing their lips together in a deep kiss that lit a fire deep inside him. Without pausing, he deepened the kiss, pressing Collin back onto the mattress as he rolled him onto his back. Tank would have asked if he was too heavy, but Collin held him tight, kissing away any chance at words.

Tank was on fire. Energy raced through him as their kisses grew more heated, and Tank tugged off the shirt Collin wore, a few threads snapping with his rough handling. But now that he had decided, there was nothing that was going to stop him.

Collin held his hands, and Tank hesitated, wondering what he'd done wrong. "We have all the time we need," he whispered. "There's no hurry. I promise you." He stroked Tank's cheek and drew their bodies back together.

Tank rubbed Collin's chest before sliding his hands around his back, cradling him in his arms. He was sleek and so warm. Tank loved the heat and drew Collin slightly upward, holding his muscular back while sliding a hand downward to cup that firm butt.

Collin did the same, slipping his hands under the band of Tank's boxers, grabbing his buttcheeks, pressing closer, encouraging Tank onward.

Tank's boxers slipped down his legs, and he kicked them off before Collin rolled them on the bed, Tank nearly falling off the side. Collin chuckled as Tank scooted to the center of the bed. Then that happy face filled his field of vision, warm hands gliding over his chest. Tank arched and groaned as Collin tweaked his nipples. "Damn...," Collin drew out softly, the sound pure sex, sending Tank soaring. He kissed Collin again before Collin slid down his chest, tongue teasing his skin to wet heat, nipples scorched with his lips and teeth. Tank could only pant and hold on as Collin stroked and licked a trail over his skin and down his belly, driving Tank out of his mind.

"I finally have you to myself," Collin whispered, a slight smile on his lips, fire burning in his eyes.

"You're trying to kill me is what you're doing." Tank whimpered as Collin teased his fingers over his hips and then around his legs. Tank's cock stretched toward his belly, throbbing with each teasing motion. Collin sure as hell knew how to draw out the ecstasy, and Tank squirmed on the bed, needing more and yet nearly overwhelmed by Collin. His mind clouded in a haze of desire that he didn't want to see through. Tank was lost, and Collin was his guide.

Collin wrapped his fingers around Tank's length, stroking and pushing Tank's desire higher. He tried to think, but Collin filled all his attention. Tank finally let go as Collin lightly cupped him, teasing some more before taking him between his lips, surrounding Tank in the wettest heat possible. He gasped and clutched the bedding while Collin sucked him into a squirming mess.

"Fuck, Tank," Collin said, and Tank couldn't help grinning. There was something weird about Collin talking like that. He always sounded so proper with that accent of his. "What?" He squeezed Tank's cock hard, and Tank groaned, squirming under the sensation.

"You...."

"Because I said fuck? How about bollocks...?" He grinned, cupping Tank's balls. "Arse...."

Tank locked gazes with Collin. "You swear like you're going to tea," Tank told him, and Collin grinned.

"Does this feel like I'm having tea?" Collin sucked him again. Damn, the man had talent, because Tank knew from his limited experience that most guys couldn't take him, and yet Collin did... all the fucking way. It was sexy as hell.

"No, but I'm never going to be able to watch British TV again without getting a boner." He chuckled, and Collin slipped off the bed and pulled off the last of his clothes. Collin was beautiful, with a smooth chest, narrow hips, and a trim body that spoke of work rather than leisure. Not that he was surprised. Collin seemed to understand the value of hard work and wasn't soft like Tank had originally expected. He stalked back toward the bed and climbed up onto the sheets. Tank looked on with rapt attention as Collin drew closer.

"Then what does this do for you?" Collin asked in a full accent that had Tank's cock throbbing. Damn, was that all it was going to take? He loved the way Collin sounded. He shivered as Collin slowly stroked his chest, fingers sliding downward. He held his breath and closed his eyes, arching his back as Collin's lips and tongue slipped over his skin. Holy hell, this was better than anything Tank could imagine, and Tank knew he was coming to the end of his control.

He pulled away and cupped Collin's cheeks in his hands, then kissed him hard with a hint of himself on Collin's tongue. "You know what they say about us cowboys?"

"No," Collin said.

"We believe in fair play," Tank said. "And standing up for our fellow man." He smiled. "Now look what's standing for me." He stroked Collin's long cock before returning the favor the very best he could. Damn, he was perfect, and Tank loved the deep groans that emanated from Collin's chest. Bobbing his head, he did his best to draw everything he could out of Collin.

"Tank," Collin moaned, shaking a little.

"I know. It's what you did to me." Tank let Collin slide from between his lips. "You drove me crazy. You have ever since you got here." He wrapped his arms around Collin, pulling them chest to chest. "You make me want things I don't think I can have."

"Why?" Collin asked.

"Because maybe I don't deserve them," Tank confessed. "Maybe I'm not the person you want to think I am."

Collin huffed and met Tank's gaze. "If this has something to do with Sullivan, I vow if he appears again, I'm going to kick his arse into next week. And I have news for you. You can want what you want from me, because I want whatever you're willing to give. Now roll over on your back."

Tank did as he was asked, and Collin straddled his legs, bringing their cocks together, then rocking his hips. Tank gave himself over to the waves of intense pleasure. Collin had magic hands and a body made for the best kind of sin.

"Collin… I…," Tank muttered as pleasure built upon delight. He gripped the bedding, trying to stay in control, but it seemed that Collin was in charge at the moment, and Tank didn't have the willpower or the desire to do a thing about it.

When Collin tweaked one of his nipples, pinching it almost to the point of pain but staying with pressure, the pleasure center in his brain went into overdrive, and Tank clamped his eyes closed as he lost the last of his hold on his own body. His release was mind-blowing. He held Collin as he joined him in the throes of passion, the two of them coming, Collin's breath mingling with Tank's before they kissed, holding each other as they settled into the sweet embrace of afterglow.

Tank barely remembered Collin cleaning them both up and then returning to the bed. Tank held Collin tight and closed his eyes, letting sleep wash over him. Collin didn't move, pressing back against him.

Collin might have said good night, but Tank wasn't sure, as he drifted off into a settled and pleasant sleep.

THERE WERE times when he wished he could sleep in, and this morning was definitely one of those. His body woke him a little after dawn. He got up and quietly left Collin to sleep, then dressed and headed out to feed all the animals and make sure the hands knew what was expected.

"Is everybody going to this barn raising?" Collin asked once Tank was done.

"Yup. We all help out. The horses and cattle will be fine for the day." His phone vibrated, and Tank checked it. "Maureen says she will have breakfast in fifteen minutes"—he raised his voice—"so everyone finish up and head on over. We're all going to need our energy for a big day ahead."

"I'll be ready to go when you are," Collin said before hurrying back inside. Tank watched him go with a smile.

"Someone's taken with our visitor," one of the men commented. Tank hardened his gaze in his direction before stalking off toward the house. He didn't like talk among the men, not about him or anyone else, and they knew it. Still, he let them wag their chins and instead went inside, where he got his work gloves and tools together.

Collin joined him at the truck about the time Tank was ready to go. "Let's go raise a barn," Collin said with a grin.

THE YARD was a hive of activity. One team of men was unloading a huge truck that sat off to the side, and another was in the process of taking down the old building off to the left behind the main barn. While there was a great deal of talking, it all seemed orderly.

"Glad you could make it," George said with a grin. "It's really different to back home."

Collin chuckled. "You even sound like a cowboy."

George took a deep breath. "I never would have thought of it, but this is my home almost as much as the estate in Northumberland. Maybe more so. There I'm the duke, my lord, the one everyone looks to. Good or bad, right or wrong, I'm the one that they all watch. But here... it's different. I'm Alan's husband, a guy who helps with the horses and chips in whenever he can." He grinned.

"Hey, Georgie, I could use your help over here," one of the men called, and he hurried over to haul away boards that had been taken down. He carried them over to the pile of what was reusable, and Collin got to work helping George.

He knew there was only so much he could do to help since he didn't have many barn construction skills. But he grabbed a wheelbarrow, and once an area had been taken down, he cleaned up the debris so that construction could start as soon as possible.

Maureen pressed a cold water bottle into his hand. "Drink something. And here. I made breakfast sandwiches." She handed Collin one of those, and he inhaled it in about three bites. She gave him another before heading on to where more of the men were working. Collin had no doubt that Maureen was more than capable of doing the work the hands were, but she seemed to show her care through food, and Collin was grateful, especially as that second sandwich with egg and bacon settled warmly in his stomach. He downed the last of the water before returning to work.

"You doing okay?" Tank asked, carrying a steel connector in each hand like they weighed nothing.

Collin nodded. "Where did all this come from?"

Tank set down the brackets, and Maureen handed him food. He thanked her and tucked in. "Alan and Maureen decided to replace the old barn with a kit building. It will go up faster, and some of the sections were preassembled." He turned as another truck arrived, this one with the wall frames and roof trusses lying on it. "All we have to do is make sure everything matches up and we can get the feed shed put together quickly." Tank was smiley, and his eyes seemed to shine. Another large truck pulled into the drive, and men climbed out. Collin was about to return to his task when Tank's expression shifted to stormy in seconds.

"What's he doing here?" Collin ground out as he saw that Sullivan stood with the men.

"They're from Pettigrew's place. I wonder if they hired him on." Tank shook his head. "He'll regret it if he did."

Collin discreetly patted Tank's arm. "Just stay away from him and don't let that arsehole pull you into any of his drama." He knew a troublemaker when he saw one, and Collin wouldn't put it past Sullivan to decide to get revenge for whatever slights he thought Tank had given him. Collin wished Tank would tell him what had happened, but he could almost feel Tank clamming up just standing next to him. Tank nodded and stomped away from Sullivan and the men he'd arrived with. Collin sighed and returned to his task, noticing that the sun didn't seem as bright as it had a few minutes earlier.

HE KEPT busy. There were always cleanup tasks that needed to be done, and Collin did all of them without complaint. "Hey," one of the men Collin didn't know called to him. "Can you give me a hand?" he asked.

"Sure, what are you doing?" Collin asked as he hurried over. "I'm Collin."

"Harry," he said, his expression serious and his attention on the task at hand. His weathered face and the touches of gray in his dark hair said he'd been around and seen a lot in his time. "We're adding the siding to the outside." He seemed nice enough. "Everything is over there, and Alan said that they are going to use as many full pieces as possible, so this should go pretty quickly. I need someone to help hold the boards in place while I attach them."

"I can do that," Collin said, his gaze shifting to Tank as he walked nearby. He was worried about him. Just by the way he held his shoulders, Collin knew something was wrong. "You came with the guys from the Pettigrew place?" he asked, not taking his gaze from Tank.

"Yeah. I do a lot of the maintenance work for him." Harry was wiry, and there was keen intelligence behind his brown eyes, like he didn't miss much. He looked around until he saw Sullivan. "Don't trust him," he warned, gesturing with his head.

Collin nodded. "What has he done?"

Harry tilted his head toward a stack of boards, and they each took an end and carried three of them to where they would be starting on the north side of the framed-up building. "Nothing yet. But I know his type. Came to the boss with some sob story." He shook his head. "There's something about him rubs me the wrong way." He started working at the base, leveling things up and marking elevations. Collin stayed close and let him do his work. "Where you from? You got an accent like George."

"Our families live pretty close to each other at home," Collin answered.

Harry nodded. "You got a title like him?" He continued working.

"Yeah, I do. Not that it matters," he added with a shrug. "I like that it doesn't here." Harry nodded and continued working.

"You doing okay?" Tank asked as he handed them each a bottle of water.

"We're good." Collin couldn't help smiling. "I'm trying to keep an eye on the unwelcome guest at the party."

Tank nodded, and Harry glowered. "You know that guy, Tank? What's he like?" The subtext in that question hung in the air.

"Just be careful of him," Tank said to Harry, then turned and left. Collin had a pretty good idea it was so Harry couldn't ask any more questions. That was Tank—hold your cards close to the vest and tell no one anything, even if they might be able to help.

Harry, on the other hand, nodded as he glanced over at Sullivan before returning to work. It was like whatever message Tank had been sending had been received and fully understood. Maybe these cowboys had a language all their own and a ton of words weren't required. Collin shook his head as Harry had him bring the first board over. He got it placed, had Collin hold it, and then made sure it was level before fastening it in place with a nail gun. He then double-checked everything before starting the detailed process on the next board.

"I gotta ask," Collin said once they had made their way around the perimeter of the new building, setting the first board in a perfectly level square.

"Shoot," Harry said while Collin held the board between the corner and the opening for the large door. He moved one corner up ever so slightly before gunning it in place.

"Okay, first thing, why did we do it that way?" It seemed like a lot of time and work with little to show for it.

"Because with the initial course set, now the other guys can start covering the different sides and we know it's all plumb and level." They returned to the north side, and when Harry directed him to another board, they picked up the pace. Collin understood why they had taken so much time now. "What else did you want to know?"

He glanced over at Tank. "Are all you cowboys so dang quiet?"

"You mean like Tank?" Harry asked before pointing to another board. Collin brought it over, and Harry measured it. "You ever used a circular saw?" Collin nodded. "Can you cut that on the line I drew?"

"Sure." Collin lifted the board.

"To answer your question—nope," Harry said. "Most guys talk and yammer like old hens. They want to talk mostly about nothing. Some complain a lot. Others you see watching, and you know they're plotting for advantage, like the new guy. Tank, he's as solid as they come, just never said too much." He measured a couple more boards and drew lines for cuts. "Not since he got home. We all think the service changed him, but it ain't none of our business. Tank's someone you can trust when the chips are down, and that's all that matters."

Collin heard the conviction in Harry's voice. It was reassuring. Part of Collin hadn't been able to help but wonder what might be behind Sullivan's accusations. Tank seemed so reluctant to just say his side of the story. Granted, with a guy like Sullivan, there didn't need to be anything. Guys like him lived in a world where everything that happened to them was someone else's fault.

"Go on and make those cuts. Then we can get started."

Collin carried the boards over to the saw table, put on the safety glasses, and carefully made the cuts.

"I take it you're a handy guy."

The hair on the back of Collin's neck stood on end. He didn't even have to turn around to know who it was. He could feel his gaze on him, and it sent a shiver up his spine.

"I bet you know your way around a lot of things." Was this guy trying to be suggestive? It wasn't working at all. Collin's stomach roiled, and he tensed as a hand rested on his back.

He held the short board he was working on in front of him as he turned around. "You keep your hands off me or I'll cut the bloody things off."

"Aren't you feisty," Sullivan said with a dark smile. "I think I like that."

Collin stepped away. He had been trained too well to cause a scene. Sullivan tried to close the distance between them again. Tank grabbed him before he could, pulling Sullivan back. He stumbled and fell on his ass on the grass.

"Hey, get your ass back to work," one of the men yelled at Sullivan, who glowered at both of them before stalking off.

"Did he hurt you?" Tank asked.

Collin brushed where Sullivan had touched him. "No, I'm fine." He wanted to hold Tank, but he stood tall, the way he'd been taught. "Thank you, though." He picked up the boards from the ground. "I need to get these back over to Harry."

Tank narrowed his eyebrows. "Did he say anything to you?" Collin shook his head. Tank was getting up a head of steam, and Collin didn't want to be the cause of an altercation. They were here to get this building put up, not fight or cause drama.

"How long do we go?" Collin asked, trying to change the subject.

"As long as the light lasts. We aren't going to finish it, but enough will be done that Maureen, Alan, and their men will be able to." He leaned closer, his musky scent filling Collin's nose. "You're sure you're okay?" he asked in a whisper. "I need to be certain."

Collin's throat caught, and he swallowed hard. Those few words told Collin just how Tank felt about him. He nodded. "I'm okay. But thank you for your help." Damn, he wanted to kiss Tank right there. Hell, he'd love to pull him behind one of the damn buildings and show Tank just how much his care and concern meant. Those were two things that Collin wasn't used to having in his life. To say his father was cold and selfish was an understatement. His mother had been the only warmth in his life, and she'd been gone a long time.

"Are you ready?" Harry asked.

"Sorry," he said and carried the boards over to where Harry was working. He set them down and took the others to cut them while Harry got those placed.

Collin knew he needed to keep his mind on what he was doing, but he still found himself glancing to where Tank was working with another of the guys to put the siding on the front of the building, around the main door. He looked so damned sexy in those jeans that hugged his ass and thighs.

He made the cuts he needed to and took the boards over to Harry, then took the next set to be cut. Saws, hammers, and nail guns sounded from all around as a near swarm of men worked on the building. A group had just finished putting the boards on the roof, and metal sheets were being cut to lay on it. The siding was going up on most of the sides, with Harry checking the other teams to make sure their work was correct. Collin cut all the pieces and helped when it came to setting up the scaffolding so they could reach the tops of the walls.

"It's happened so fast," Collin said to Alan when he had a few minutes' break. He had never worked so hard in his life. It seemed like he hadn't stopped all day.

"It really has. The basic building will be up by the end of the day. None of the finishing work inside has been done, but we can take a little more time with that." He lifted his gaze. "There are hamburgers and hot dogs on the grill. Head on around to the patio in back if you get hungry." It was clear that everyone was feeling the urgency as the day quickly came to a close.

"Thanks, but I've got to get some more boards cut for Harry." He shared a smile with Alan and hurried back to make the cuts Harry needed and set the pieces that were done on the platform at his feet. At some point during the day, Harry had shifted to simply giving him a list of measurements, and Collin had been cutting the siding to fit.

"This is the last for this side," Harry said as he handed Collin the scraps of wood. Collin cut them and helped Harry put the last pieces into place like they were finishing a giant jigsaw puzzle. Just as Collin was about to get down, he felt the scaffolding begin to move. He slipped over the side and down onto the ground and steadied it as Harry put in the last nails.

"Get down," Collin told Harry as the pressure on his arms increased. "Now!" he cried, and Harry slipped down the other side. As soon as he hit the ground, Collin backed away. First one piece fell, and then the entire short structure collapsed in a clang of piping and loose boards. "Jesus."

"Is everyone okay?" Alan called as a group of guys raced over.

Tank had Collin in his arms before he could answer. "I'm fine. What about Harry?" Collin asked just before he saw him with some of the others. He seemed okay, though.

"Who built the platform?" Alan asked.

"Harry and Chip worked on it," Collin answered as Alan went through the pile on the ground. He picked up a few pieces, frowning, and then set them aside. He then went over and checked the scaffoldings on the remaining sides, testing them.

"Are they okay?" Harry asked, going behind Alan.

"They seem to be," Alan said before the two of them talked quietly together. Then the men got back to work after first testing the platforms. Theirs had only been about four feet off the ground, but still, he or Harry could have been hurt.

Tank took his hand, and Collin found himself half pulled away and into the barn. The horses peered over their stall walls, curious about the strangers who had entered their domain. "Are you sure you're okay?" Tank asked, running his hands over him.

"Yes." He was okay, but his legs felt shaky as he thought about what could have happened. "But what went wrong with the scaffolding platform? It was fine for the last few hours."

"If they aren't built correctly...," Tank began.

Collin stepped back, his hands on his hips, and looked into Tank's eyes. "Your eyes wander when you're trying to avoid something. I've seen it every time Sullivan is around and I see it now. There's something you aren't telling me."

"It looked to me like some of the bracing pipes had been loosened or maybe removed. Alan looked them over, and they weren't attached anymore. They were on the ground."

Collin swallowed. "I saw a pipe under the platform the last time I brought Harry the cuts, but I didn't think anything of it. Maybe I should have said something."

Tank growled. "I need to talk to Alan, but did you see anyone near where you were working?"

Collin shrugged. "Lots of people. Remember, there were men everywhere. It was like a cowboy college reunion out there." He had hoped to come up with something funny to make light of what happened, but it fell flat.

Tank tugged him into a hug. "At least you're okay. That's what's important." They both took a deep breath. "We should go see what we can do to finish up." He hurried toward the door.

"Tank," Collin said, "I'm okay, and nothing bad happened, other than a mess on the ground."

He strode back. "But you could have been hurt, and if someone did sabotage the platform, then I need to find out who it is." He seemed so earnest.

Collin took his hand. "*We* need to figure it out. You and I." He suddenly wondered if he was talking about the platform or the two of them, but Tank smiled slightly and nodded. Collin slipped his arms around Tank's neck. "If someone did this maliciously, then we already have a prime suspect. Maybe have a talk with a few of the other guys. They might have seen something. Then we can make sure Harry knows what happened."

"And Pettigrew will fire his sorry ass," Tank added. "Maybe we can get him to run Sullivan out of town."

"Do people actually do that?" Collin asked.

Tank shook his head and kissed him hard until Collin's vision swam, before backing away. The last thing they wanted was to be caught kissing in the barn, though Collin was wondering what he'd have to do to get a roll in the hay. Judging by the bulge in Tank's jeans… not too damned much, if he played his cards right.

CHAPTER 9

ALAN CALLED a halt to the work. "There's plenty of food and drink for everyone," he added as the guys hurried to stow their tools in the trucks before filing around to the patio. Chip manned the grill, and Maureen carried out bowls of salads and sides. It was quite a production as everyone lined up, filled plates, and then sat down. Tank couldn't ever remember a gathering of almost thirty people that was this quiet with everyone eating.

"We got the outside of the building done," Collin said, bumping against Tank's shoulder. "I've watched shows on telly where they build a house in a day, but I never thought I'd see it." He returned to eating, and once he was done, he leaned against Tank's side with a yawn that he tried to stifle.

"We'll get ready to go soon," Tank said, and Collin nodded.

Tank finished eating. Then they gathered up their things and said goodbyes, receiving hugs from Maureen and Alan, as well as Chip, before heading back to the ranch.

Collin went right inside, but Tank checked the barn and made sure the horses had water and feed. Then he went into the house, where he let the dogs outside. They were all excited to see him, and Tank played with all three of them before heading to his room. Collin lay on the bed, breathing evenly. "You did really good today."

"Thank you," Collin mumbled.

"I know it was a lot, and you held in there to the end." Tank went to the bathroom and started the water, then stepped under the shower. There was no way he was going to go to bed dirty.

He had planned a quick clean, but Collin slipped in behind him and wrapped his arms around Tank's waist. He didn't say anything, and Tank maneuvered him under the water before grabbing the soap to lather his hands. The fact that Collin was half asleep on his feet was no surprise.

Tank washed him gently, stroking his chest and back. "Oh, Tank…," Collin mumbled, "that's good." His legs trembled as Tank ran his soapy hands over them. Then he turned Collin around and ran his big hands over his smooth back and down past the curve, filling his palms with Collin's pale, firm buttcheeks. Then he stood and tugged Collin to him, back to chest, holding him up as the water washed over them both. He gently stroked Collin's chest and over his flat belly.

"It seems not all of you is sleepy," Tank whispered, slipping his fingers over Collin's balls and then along his upright shaft. After grabbing the soap, he lathered up once again and turned Collin out of the water before stroking along his length. Collin leaned back against him and slipped his hand behind him, gripping Tank's throbbing cock. He didn't stroke but held it tight as Tank continued his motions.

"God, Tank," Collin said as he stood still. "I can barely move."

"Then let me take care of us." Tank kissed his shoulder, then tweaked a nipple as he stroked harder. Collin shook in his arms and gasped before stiffening from head to toe, coming over Tank's hand in a nearly silent explosion.

Collin sighed softly and seemed to lose the last of his energy. Tank rinsed him off, letting the water run over both of them for a minute. Then he turned it off and grabbed towels, wrapping Collin in one before quickly drying himself. Collin got himself dried off, and Tank hung up the towels. "Go climb into bed. I'll be there in a minute."

Collin left the bathroom, and Tank thought about jerking off. Having Collin in his arms like that, giving over his pleasure completely, was so hot, and Tank had loved it. There was something about the trust in that action that really set his heart racing. Collin's trust was important and something he wanted to keep.

Tank pushed thoughts of Sullivan and his accusations to the back of his mind. A single thought of that man was enough to send his dick running for cover. He turned out the bathroom light and went into the dark bedroom. The pups were all curled up in their bed, and Tank slipped into his own. Collin snuggled up to him, and Tank held him tightly.

"You're a good man, Tank," Collin mumbled and then seemed to sink more deeply into slumber.

Tank's mind tried to put up a fight, but he was too tired and gave himself over to exhaustion. He wasn't sure what to do about Sullivan, and he couldn't help wondering if that bastard had weakened the work platform. If he had, what was he trying to accomplish? The answers weren't going to come tonight, and Tank finally slipped into an uneasy sleep. Leaving things unsettled ate at him. Tank liked things wrapped up neatly. But this was becoming more of a mess as time went by.

TANK HAD been working for a couple of hours before he saw any sign that Collin was up. He caught up on the work that had been left from the day before and rode out to check on the herd. The men were coming in late because of the super long day yesterday, but Tank knew there were things to do.

His ranch wasn't huge, but there was always work, and letting some things go for a day was fine, but more than that and it was too easy to get behind.

"You never stop."

Tank stepped out of the equipment shed after putting the ATV away. He knew Sullivan's voice before he saw him striding over. "You know I never do."

"Yeah. You'll do anything to get rid of me and try to keep me quiet." Sullivan stepped closer, his eyes wild, and Tank wondered what the hell had happened to him. His hands shook, and he seemed pale, yet wired all to hell. Tank took a step back, instinctively wanting distance. "I worked hard yesterday, and you got me fired."

"I did no such thing," Tank said.

"You and your friends," Sullivan spat.

Tank felt his anger rise, but he kept it under control. "And you damaged the work platform." That was a bluff. He didn't know for sure, but there had been a message from Alan that morning that Sullivan had been seen hanging around the platform when he should have been working elsewhere. "What I want to know is why?" He hoped if he acted like it was common knowledge, then maybe Sullivan would cop to it.

"I...."

Tank drew closer, smelling weakness. Sullivan had always been a weasel, and Tank wondered what redeeming qualities he had ever seen in him. The idea that he had entertained getting involved with him all those years ago turned his stomach. "I know what you did. There were too many people around. Why the fuck would you do something like that? People could have been hurt."

"Like I got hurt," Sullivan yelled as he lunged at Tank, who stepped out of the way. Sullivan overbalanced and ended up flat on his face in the dirt. "You were supposed to have my back. You were supposed to fucking care."

Tank leaned down. "I was following orders, and you went off on your own."

"You were supposed to care for me," Sullivan said. "You should have thought of me first." He scrambled to his feet. "I was the one who should have come first," he reiterated and squared his shoulders. "But Tank puts no one before himself. Your little boyfriend in there will figure that out soon enough, and when he does…." He grinned stupidly, but Tank was tired of trying to figure Sullivan out. "I want to be there to see that."

Tank shook his head. He had wondered just how twisted the reality had gotten in Sullivan's mind, and now he knew. "You need to get yourself some help."

"Yeah, you do," Collin said firmly as he turned the corner. He stopped with his arms folded over his chest. "What the hell were you thinking with that little stunt you pulled? Harry was nearly hurt. Why would you do that?"

Sullivan narrowed his gaze at Collin. "Harry wasn't the target."

"Me?" Collin asked, his eyes widening. Tank stepped to the side, getting between them. He didn't want Sullivan even *looking* at Collin.

"Get the fuck off my land and never set foot here again." He swore if Sullivan pulled anything, he'd rip the man apart.

Sullivan seemed to be reaching the end of his rope. The man was a snake, and Tank was well aware of when they were at their most dangerous. He stood his ground, but Sullivan's eyes grew even wider and wilder. Tank braced himself, expecting Sullivan to rush at him. But instead he pulled a knife, and Tank backed up. He was even crazier than Tank had first suspected.

"Don't you even want to know why?" Sullivan asked with an unhinged grin. "Huh?" He seemed to be directing this to Collin, which Tank thought strange. What business could Sullivan have with him?

"What did I ever do to you, other than become friends with Tank?" Collin asked.

Tank kept an eye on Sullivan as the man lunged forward. Tank backed away and dodged his clumsy motion, watching the knife.

"Is that what you think?" Sullivan asked. "It's not hard to get work finding people or delivering messages." He took another swipe, and Tank jumped back just as Collin raced around him. Collin knocked Sullivan's feet out from under him with a beautiful roundhouse kick, sending him flying and landing flat on his back with a thud that had to hurt. The knife skittered away on the grass, and Tank moved it away, not wanting to touch it. That way the sheriff could use it as evidence.

"Collin, stay back," Tank snapped, but Collin already had Sullivan by the collar.

"What did you mean?" he asked, shaking him slightly. "I spent six years at an all-boys boarding school. I know how to defend myself, and I certainly know half a million ways to make you hurt. The bullies at Eton were experts, and I learned from the best." He grabbed Sullivan's nipple and gave it a merciless twist.

"Fuck!" Sullivan shouted.

"You think that hurt? Wait until I do it three or four more times." He repeated the motion, and Sullivan tried to pull away, struggling like crazy. "Now what the hell did you mean?" Collin leaned closer. "I can squeeze your bollocks until you scream in terror." Collin gave Sullivan's chest another twist. Tears ran down Sullivan's cheeks. "Now tell me."

"I do favors for people. Paid favors, and it didn't take your father very long to find out where you were staying. He wanted someone to cause some trouble and get you to come back home. The fact that you were staying at Tank's was just a happy accident for me. Sort of a twofer."

Collin pushed Sullivan back down to the ground. "My father sent you here?" he asked. "What the hell for?"

Sullivan propped himself up on his elbows. "He doesn't like having a poof for a son—his words. And he was looking for someone to keep an eye out and make enough trouble here that you went home. It seems Daddy has someone he wants you to marry." Sullivan sneered. "Like a queer like you was going to marry a woman." He rolled his eyes. "I took the crazy man's money and did what he asked. Then I found out that you and old Timmy here were shacking up, and suddenly the job didn't seem so bad." He tried to get up, but Collin kept him down using the heel of his boot in the center of his chest.

Collin seemed livid, and Tank worried he'd do something he'd regret. "He isn't worth it," Tank said and tugged Collin back. "I'm going to call the sheriff, and he can pick him up. I'll press charges for him coming at me with a knife, and then Sheriff Donaldson can deal with him." At the very least, he'd be behind bars.

"Yes, sure," Collin said softly. "But we should also check that everything is okay. This arsehole has probably been causing trouble before he found you. God knows what he did." Collin held Sullivan down as Tank made his call.

The men began arriving and seemed amused by the man Collin kept on the ground. They looked at Collin with a certain amount of respect and went about checking on everything. *Damned gates were open*, one of the men reported through text. *Closed them. Checking for escapees.*

Tank sent a thank-you and glowered at Sullivan. "You know, you were a failure as a soldier. You always thought you knew best and listened to no one. You still think you know what you're doing. If you got hurt, it was no one's fault but your own." Tank looked at Collin. "We were in a firefight and ordered to back out to get a better position. I followed orders. Sullivan here decided to go his own way. He was shot, and I ended up going in to pull him out, though the asshole doesn't remember any of that. All he thinks is that I left him out there." Tank leaned over Sullivan and flipped him the bird. "You were a dick all those years ago, and you still are today." Damn, that felt good. He was so tired of taking shit from him.

"Why didn't you say so before?" Collin asked. "The only shame in this story is his."

"We're supposed to have each other's back. I know that, and so does he."

Collin shook his head. "That's bullshit. Where was his back-watching when he went out on his own and put everyone in danger? Answer that one for me." Tank thought he was going to spit on Sullivan. "You are so messed up that you can't even see the truth, can you? And how do you get these jobs of yours? Place an advert on some website, maybe Assholes for Hire?"

Sirens sounded, and Tank went out into the drive, met the sheriff, and led him back to where Collin waited. "Step away from him, please," the sheriff said, clearly amused.

"Of course," Collin said with as upper-crust an accent as Tank had ever heard.

"And you are?" the sheriff asked Collin as he cuffed Sullivan. "I know who *he* is. I already got a report from Pettigrew, as well as Maureen up the road. Your actions have become quite well known."

"And he confessed to damaging the scaffolding platform. Both Tank and I heard it." Damn, Collin was impressive. "To answer your question, I'm Collin Northington, Viscount Haferton, heir to the Earl of Doddington. You may call me Collin if you like."

"Well, your viscountness, can you tell me what happened?"

"Tank will. He was here longer than I was," Collin said. Tank took over, letting Collin fill in some details that Tank might have missed. "The knife he pulled is over there. We kicked it away and haven't touched it." He turned to Collin, who nodded.

"It also seems that my father might have hired him to cause trouble here," Collin told the sheriff. "I'm afraid he's still in England, so getting to him is going to be difficult."

The sheriff's eyes boggled. "I see."

"But any evidence you gather to that effect can be presented when I return." Damn, Collin was smart. If the sheriff uncovered anything, Collin could use it as leverage with his father. Maybe even get the miserable old man in trouble with the law. After all, what kind of man hired someone to scare his son just to try to get him to come home?

"I don't know if I can do that."

"I can get the local police in touch with you so you can handle things police officer to police officer. That's up to you."

"Well, we'll see what we find." The sheriff got Sullivan off the ground and into the back of his car. "I'll need a statement from each of you." He asked questions of both Tank and Collin. They answered them and gave him all the information they had. Finally the sheriff left with Sullivan, and Tank could finally relax.

"At least we know what Sullivan was up to," Tank said.

"No, we don't. Not entirely. Sullivan gave us part of the story, but there are a bunch of questions that need answers. Until yesterday Sullivan didn't actually do anything. He hung around and was a bigmouth arsehole, but that isn't going to get me to return home. He got the scaffolding to collapse, but that wasn't going to send me home either. So whatever he said, there's more to it than that."

Tank shook his head. "I don't understand."

"Neither do I," Collin said softly, but then he headed toward the house. Tank wished he knew what Collin meant, but maybe it was Collin's turn to play it close to the vest.

CHAPTER 10

WITH SULLIVAN out of the way, the next few days were quiet. Collin and Tank settled into a routine, and he found himself moving to Tank's schedule. Collin began getting up earlier to work with Tank. They repaired one of the stalls and mended a leaky shed roof, and in the afternoons, Collin worked with Barney, who was making good progress. He was still skittish, but the horse was coming to trust him, and that was good. Collin didn't think he would ever be able to be ridden. That was probably beyond Barney's ability at this point. But if he calmed down enough for breeding, then he'd be a good addition to the ranch.

"He's looking good," Tank said as Collin brought the training session to an end. He had tried to use Barney's natural equine curiosity against him, and it was really working. Each little task was met with a reward, and Collin was gentle with him, letting Barney run and work out his anxiety rather than penning it up.

Collin led Barney over to where Tank stood, coaxing him with soft words when he hesitated. "There are still some issues." He held Barney in place a little ways from Tank, who held out a carrot. "Just stay still. I really want him to take it on his own." Collin gently patted Barney's neck, and after a few seconds, he came up and munched the carrot. Tank put out another one, and Barney took that one as well. Then it was Tank's turn to gently pat his neck.

"You are a good boy," Tank crooned and smiled. This was something Collin hadn't thought possible when he first started working with Barney, but he'd hoped. The horse had been all fear and wildness, but now he had settled a lot.

"He is. And given care and some attention, he'll be a good addition to your operation. He certainly has the bloodline to be bred."

Tank nodded slowly. "Let's get him inside. He's earned his oats today." Tank backed away, and Collin felt his eyes on him as he led the horse off.

He had been here a little over a week, and things on the ranch seemed much brighter. Collin wondered what Tank was going to do when he left. They had only six more days together, and then Alan, George, and Collin were returning to England. Tank would be alone once more. Collin had spent years on his own, and that had been fine. But there was a difference between being alone and being lonely, and Collin knew that once he went home, Tank was probably going to be the latter. Heck, Collin was going to miss the huge guy like a lost tooth. Not many things scared him, but that sent a cold wave up his back, even though it was hot and getting warmer under the bright July sun. Collin knew there was nothing he could do about it, though. He had his life back in England, and Tank had his here. He couldn't ask Tank to give up his family legacy any more than Collin could let go of his.

There were times Collin wished he could simply walk away, say to hell with it all, and build a life of his own.

Collin put Barney into his stall and made sure he had plenty to eat and drink. He stroked him gently before closing the door behind him. Being here on the ranch was wonderful, and he loved being able to get away from his pain-in-the-arse father for a while. But he had obligations he couldn't walk away from. The people on the estate needed him to make sure that his father didn't let everything go to wrack and ruin. They depended on the place for their livelihood, and when things got tough, his father would simply cut back rather than trying to grow their operations. That kind of thinking was something his father had never been able to do. Ever since he turned eighteen, Collin had been the one to see to it that the actual business was being conducted properly. It had been a lot to take on, but Collin had realized that if he didn't, there would be nothing left once his father was done.

"What has you so deep in thought?" Tank asked. Collin realized he'd been standing there staring at a bale of hay.

"I've got six more days," Collin said softly before sighing. "I know I can't stay, but I wish I could." He swallowed hard. "I like it here." He tugged Tank down into a kiss. "And I like you." That was the real crux of what was happening. Collin had come to the US to try to find a man like Alan, and instead he'd found someone different—Tank. Now, if he had met a cowboy, maybe they could have resettled in England together. But no, he'd met a man as tied to the land here as Collin was there. "I wish you could come back with me."

Tank swallowed hard, nodding slightly. "Do you think your friends would like a rough guy like me?"

"My friends like Alan. Everyone knows him. He's made quite a name for himself there." Collin looked around the barn. "I know it's a stupid idea, though." If there was only a way to pick up the ranch and everyone to move them near home.

"We've known each other for little over a week," Tank said.

Collin nodded. "I know. It's stupid to get my heart all tied up in knots." He knew very well that going home would be one of the most difficult things he had ever done. But his mother had taught him that he had a duty to the family and to the estate. He couldn't simply turn his back on that.

"I understand, because I feel the same way. We've spent most of our time together since you arrived." Tank sighed and sat down on a bale of hay across the aisle. "I've spent the last few years since getting out of the service on my own. Sullivan tried to bring charges against me, that I had abandoned him on the battlefield. It didn't hold water, but guys thought there could be some truth to it. So I wasn't trusted, and I left as soon as my time was up. I once thought Sullivan was my friend, but I didn't know after that." He hung his head, and Collin sat next to him, taking his hand.

Collin didn't say anything; he simply wanted Tank to know that he was there for him. Gently, he stroked Tank's work-roughened palm. "I'm sorry."

"Don't be," Tank said more forcefully. "The last thing I want from you is pity or you to feel sorry for me. I don't think I can take that. Not from you." Collin nodded and wished he'd followed his initial instinct and kept quiet. "After years in the service, I came home. My dad was still running the ranch, but he was having trouble and had for a while. The herd was almost gone, and he was leasing out land to try to bring in some money. I worked hard, brought back the herds, started breeding horses, and plowed every cent I had into the ranch. Things were just turning around when Dad died." Tank squeezed his hand. "After that, I...."

"Grew quiet and figured you were the only person you could really rely on," Collin supplied, and Tank nodded. "You poured your energy into the ranch and keeping this place going."

"That's about it. I thought I didn't need anything else, and then along comes this high-and-mighty British viscount...." He pronounced it like it rhymed with *discount*, which made Collin smile. "I thought he was going to be a stick-in-the-mud, but I was wrong." Tank swallowed hard, and Collin leaned against him. Tank released his hand and slipped an arm around him, drawing Collin tighter.

"What are we going to do?" Collin asked.

"I don't know. Make the most of the time we have. You're going to have to go home and deal with your father, because anyone who hires someone like Sullivan just isn't right in the head."

"No. And that's got me wondering what else he's been up to." Collin would figure all that out when he returned. He had thought about calling his father to talk to him, but that just made his stomach churn. His father would only spout his usual selfishness and make Collin worry. Whatever was waiting for him would be there when he returned. "But I'm not going to let him throw a wet blanket over things." His father also knew how to get in touch with him. "And yeah, I have six more days. Let's make them special." He leaned closer and kissed Tank.

A throat clearing made Collin pull away. "Sorry, boss. I didn't know you were getting busy in here." Denny's smile was wicked.

Tank growled, and the smile vanished in an instant.

"Tank," Collin said.

"What do you want, Denny?" he asked.

"Where did you want us to move the south group of cattle? You said you were concerned they might be overgrazing." He was a younger man, but he had intelligent eyes.

"Bring them north to the next range," Tank told him, and Denny hurried out of the barn. "Do you want to help move some cattle?"

"Seriously?" Collin asked.

"Yeah. You can work with some of the herd today, and tomorrow we're going to Cheyenne to the rodeo. Alan and George got tickets, and the four of us are going. Did you forget?"

"I think I did." Collin had lost track of the days. He stood up. "Let me get my gloves and I'll meet you outside with the guys." He hurried inside and got himself set for work. Then he made sure the dogs had food and water before joining Tank in the yard. Tank was already on the ATV, and Collin jumped on behind him and they took off.

"I have to ask," he said over the purr of the engine. "Does this make me a real cowboy?"

"We'll see," Tank told him as the other men joined them, all of them zipping across the land.

"You know, these things sort of kill the mystique." Collin hung on tightly, loving being this close to Tank.

"Maybe, but it gets the work done faster," Tank yelled back as they approached the large swing gate. The men ahead of them opened it wide, and they all passed through. One of them veered off to the left and got off, then took up at position near the gate, while the rest fanned out around the back side of the herd. Then they got in a line and began moving forward.

The cattle seemed a little curious, looking up from their feeding. Tank pulled to a stop and climbed off. "What do you want me to do?" Collin asked.

"Take over here and stay in line with the other men." Tank walked between the vehicles, waving his arms and yelling. As they drew closer, the herd began to move toward the gate. The cowboys took it slow, and they continued moving the herd forward, some of them calling out.

This seemed really easy, and Collin smiled, pleased he could help. Just as they crested the rise near the gate, some of the cattle decided to go right. Collin veered off, revving the engine, and they second-guessed themselves, rejoining the rest of the group going through the gate. Once all the cattle were through, the gate was swung shut with a loud clang.

"There are stragglers. Go round them up and get them to join the rest."

Denny saluted Tank, and the men took off back through the gate.

"You did good," Tank said once the others were gone. "Real good."

"It seemed like the right thing to do. The others were moving, and I hoped that if I got them turned, they'd follow in the end." Collin pulled up next to Tank, who climbed on behind him. "What's next?" He revved the engine, and Tank laughed gently in his ear.

"Water. Let's check." He pointed and then held on, and they were off.

Collin loved to drive, and without any roads, he didn't have to worry about left or right. He did follow Tank's directions and came to a secondary watering hole.

"Where does this come from?" he asked.

"The same creek as the other. All we did here was run a few pipes in and out so it creates a watering station." Tank checked the water before climbing back on. "It's good. I like to make sure that the water is flowing in and out, not stagnant." He pointed back toward the house, but Collin wasn't ready to go in yet. Instead, he pointed the ATV toward the creek, using the trees as a guide. "I take it you have something else in mind."

Collin glided to a stop. "Is that okay? We can go back."

Tank pointed toward the trees, and they were off once again.

It was hot, and the sun seemed merciless to a guy from northern England. As soon as they slid under the trees, cooler air washed over him, and Collin felt like he could breathe again. Near the water, he pulled to a stop and turned off the engine. Getting down, he slipped off his hat and then his shirt. At the water's edge, the boots, jeans, and his underwear followed, and then he waded bare-assed into the chill water—but after three steeps, he slipped and fell into a hole.

Collin came up sputtering to Tank laughing from the bank. He frowned and then sent up a wall of water in Tank's direction. It didn't reach him, and Tank continued laughing.

"Are you going to join me?" Collin turned around, closed his eyes, and went under, the water cold but refreshing after the heat out in the open. When he came up, Tank stood shirtless in the same place, and Collin found himself breathless… because, damn. Tank was stunning, with his wide bare shoulders and thick chest. Collin walked to the shallows and then out of the water, not taking his gaze away from Tank. He got a smile, and then Tank came closer, crooking a finger in his direction. Collin came up to him and stood on the bank as Tank pulled him into his arms.

He loved petting the man. Tank was all muscle, and the black hair on his chest contrasted with the fact that Collin had none. He splayed his fingers, letting the slight roughness pass under them. Tank hugged him tightly, his lips working the base of Collin's neck as Collin used his lips and tongue on one of Tank's pert nipples.

Tank groaned—a lovely, sexy sound that sent a pure wave of passion running through Collin. He wanted Tank badly, and when Tank lifted him, Collin wrapped his legs around Tank's waist, a huge hand supporting his ass as he kissed Tank with everything he had. "I want you, Tank. I want to feel you inside," Collin whispered, loving how Tank quivered at his words.

"Not here," Tank managed to whisper. "It's too rough."

Collin was almost too far gone to care, but Tank gently got him down on his feet. Collin breathed deeply, his entire body revved into high gear. He was so ready for Tank, he didn't care where they were.

"That grass there is sharp, and I don't have anything for us to lie on." Tank reached down and picked up Collin's slacks, then handed them to him.

Now Collin felt like a fool. He yanked them on and pulled on his socks and boots before shrugging on his shirt. He had basically thrown himself at Tank and been rejected.

Tank pulled him into another hug. "Sweetheart, it's just till I can get you back in the house." He slipped his rough hands over Collin's cheeks. "I won't have anything happen to you or let you get hurt. This is the west, and even this close to the house, there are still wild things that can be dangerous, especially near the water."

"Huh," Collin said.

"We love the water and rely on it. So do other animals, including snakes and other inhospitables. Not to mention the fact that making love on the bare ground is not at all as romantic as the idea. Taking a roll in the hayloft is just as bad. I know they show it on television and in movies, but that stuff is pokey, and it's the last thing you want to feel on your bare backside." He smiled. "Now let's finish getting dressed so we can go to the house, and I'll show you just how much I want you too." Tank kissed him hard and then released him to pull on his shirt.

Tank took control and drove them back. Denny met them and explained that all of the cattle were accounted for. "But we seem to have picked up three head."

"What? How?" Tank asked. "Are they Maureen's?"

"No. She has all her cattle tagged the way ours are. So does everyone else around here."

Tank seemed confused. "What did you do with them?"

"I kept them separate from the rest of the herd. We found them as a group in the far east of the area. There's that depression where there might have been a water hole years ago. They were down in there," Denny told him.

Tank seemed perplexed, and Collin wondered what the heck could be happening.

"Good." Tank turned on the ATV. "Go on inside. I need to figure this out."

"I'm going with you," Collin declared and climbed on behind Tank, holding tight. "Let's go." He nearly lost his hat as Tank took off, his body filled with tension. Tank seemed to know exactly where Denny was talking about, and after about fifteen minutes, he found the cattle in question.

"They look underweight to me," Collin said once Tank pulled to a stop. The three head of mostly black cattle blinked at them from the other side of a corral. It seemed strange for this sort of small area to be way out here. "What is this?"

"Separation area. Dad built it for quarantine purposes years ago when there was a disease scare. Stay here." Tank got off the ATV and walked over to where the cattle stood. He looked them over without touching them and seemed to give them a wide berth. Then he pulled his phone out of his pocket and made a call. Collin couldn't hear what he said, but his posture was tense as all hell.

"What's going on?" Collin asked.

Tank held up a finger and made another call. Once he was done, he returned to the ATV. "These cattle are sick, and we're damned lucky they didn't get mixed in with the rest of the herd." His hand shook. "I called the vet and told him where they are." He climbed back on, and as soon as Collin had a good grip, Tank was off like a bat out of hell. It was all Collin could do to hang on, and he was never so happy as when they got back to the house again.

"I called Doc Hasper, and he's on his way out," Tank told Denny. "Those cattle are sick. You can see it in their eyes and the way they seem unsteady on their feet. They've also had their tags removed. I could see where they had once been attached to their ears."

"Jesus," Denny said softly. "I kept the men away from them and handled those three myself. The other guys dealt with the rest of the strays. If they're sick, the rest of the herd didn't seem to be, and they can't have been there very long. There is no water in that depression, and they were the only ones that weren't ours and the only ones in the gully. They must have gotten into that gully right away, because they weren't mixed in with the herd."

Tank nodded as Collin's mind raced to process what he was hearing. "Are you saying that someone tried to put these three sick head of cattle in with your herd?" Collin asked. "That could...." He put his hand over his mouth at the idea that someone would do that to try to infect Tank's herd. "That's despicable."

"Yes, it is. Doc Hasper will be here soon, and he'll be able to tell what's wrong with them."

Still, Collin could see the way Tank paled and knew this could be very bad. Tank paced the area, and Collin bit his nails, something that had been trained out of him years ago. Finally, the vet arrived, and Tank took him out to the cattle while Collin headed inside to wait and worry.

CHAPTER 11

THE THREE head of cattle seemed miserable by the time Tank returned to them. Doc Hasper took one look, brought out his gun, and shot them on the spot. "I'm going to take some samples, and then I can call someone to haul these away and dispose of them safely."

"What do you think it is?" Tank asked, already fearing the worst.

Doc Hasper sighed. "If I didn't know better, I'd say anthrax. All the cattle in the area are vaccinated, so I'm wondering where these came in from. You and your boys have been vaccinated, right?" he asked, and Tank nodded. Then it hit him hard.

"Everyone except Collin," Tank said. "Son of a bitch!" He wanted to scream. "I'm going to squeeze the life out of the asshole that did this, then resuscitate him so I can kill the piece of shit again." He stormed away, swearing up a storm. He snatched his hat off his head, wanting to beat the shit out of someone, but the person he thought was responsible was already in jail. Maybe if he asked nicely, the sheriff would give him five minutes. That was all he needed to make sure Sullivan paid for this.

"The new guy I just met?" Doc Hasper asked.

"He's a guest here on the ranch. He came to visit with George and Alan." And since he didn't work with cattle, there wasn't much chance that he'd had a vaccine. "Fuck."

"Okay. Let's not get ahead of ourselves. I'm going to get these samples run as fast as I can."

"And I need to talk to the sheriff," Tank said, still fuming, his mind running in a million directions. He made his call while the vet took his samples and made a call of his own. The sheriff said he would meet both of them at the house. All Tank could see was a very black day stretching ahead of him.

"YOU HAVE got to be kidding me," Maureen snapped at dinner as Tank told everyone what they had been able to find out.

"I wish I were. Three head with anthrax were let loose in my field."

"But that doesn't make sense. All our cattle are vaccinated, and so are yours," Alan said. "What's the point? That sort of thing was a dirty trick pulled in the old days to run a rival out of business. But it doesn't make sense today." Alan set down his fork and turned to George. "Shit."

"Exactly," Tank said. "We're vaccinated as well, because we work with cattle every day." Tank looked at Collin and George. "They aren't. I never touched or came close to those cattle, but I scrubbed myself as soon as I got done with the doc and sheriff."

"The sheriff had me tested," Collin said. "And the doctor was already here. He gave George and me some treatment pills just in case and vaccinated us. We're doing what we can, but it's not going to take effect that soon." He sounded heartbroken, and Tank knew exactly how he felt.

"What I want to know is where someone got three head of unvaccinated cattle and exposed them to anthrax before putting them on your land, and how would they do that without exposing themselves to the disease?" Maureen shook her head.

"The sheriff is looking into the whole incident. But no one has reported any cattle missing, and some of those large operations would write off three head as a loss and move on."

"Do you think Sullivan is behind this?" Collin asked.

"I do," Tank said. "One of the things he said he was hired to do was to try to scare you into going home. The scaffolding incident was clumsy at best, and I doubt that was going to work. But a scare like this?" He swallowed hard. "To potentially expose you to a disease you don't have an immunity to?" That was absolutely frightening.

"George too," Alan said. "What are we going to do?"

George swallowed and set down his fork. "I'm not letting some piece of dirt run me off. What about you, Collin?"

Tank loved how Collin squared his shoulders. "We're made of sterner stuff than that." They shared a nod, a show of joint determination.

"Exactly." They raised their beer glasses in a silent toast. "Now I say we roast this Sullivan."

Tank hoped that was some British saying, though an image of Sullivan on a spit did make him smile. "The sheriff is trying to track down the cattle and will definitely be having a talk with Sullivan, as well as going through his stuff. The man isn't the brightest bulb on the string, so he'd be dumb enough to keep something that could tie him to this. In the meantime, we make sure that George and Collin don't come in direct contact with the cattle."

Collin smacked his shoulder. "Yours are all vaccinated, and so are Maureen's. These three are an anomaly, and they have been dealt with. The sheriff is going to find out the source of the issue, and that will be that. We've taken preventative measures and have the doctor's direct number." Collin leaned closer. "I know you're worried, but I'm okay, and you don't need to get your knickers in a twist."

Tank shivered and whispered into Collin's ear. Collin turned completely red and then glared at him for a second. "Later," Tank added, and Collin nodded before taking a huge drink of beer.

"What did you say to him?" Chip asked.

"Never you mind," Maureen scolded. "And you behave at my table, Timmy Rogers."

Tank grew serious. "Yes, ma'am." Everyone grew quiet until Alan and Chip chuckled. Tank lifted his gaze and found Maureen watching him, smiling a little. "You got me," he said as Maureen patted his hand.

Collin snickered next to him and shook his head. "I can't quite get over you as a Timmy."

"That's what we called him when we were kids," Alan said. "Can you imagine Tank here at ten years old? He was skinny and short. So many times, we thought the wind was going to blow him away. Then later, he grew up and then out." Alan grinned. "I barely recognized you when you got back from the Army."

"I know that's where you got your nickname," Collin said.

Tank sighed. "In a way. See, I was still this skinny kid when I enlisted, and I took shit for it. The other guys in the unit started calling me Tiny Tim. I laughed at first, but then one of them tried to pull some shit and I clocked him in the nose. Got called in for it too, but the other men were honest and came forward to explain that I was defending myself." He tried not to let the darkness of those memories wash over him. "He got discharged for his conduct, and I was excused. And then one of the men started calling me Tank. Don't know why, but after that I grew into the name. I guess you could say that I hit a major growth spurt. Nothing fit, and I was going through clothes by the ton. They issued me four sets of uniforms in a year. I was taller and a hell of a lot stronger. I was nineteen, maybe twenty." He pushed his plate away, and Collin rubbed his hand under the table.

"When are we going to the rodeo?" Collin asked out of the blue, changing the subject as he laced their fingers together and Tank let his story taper off. He hated talking about his time overseas and was grateful that Collin understood that. "I'm really looking forward to it."

And just like that, the conversation veered off into arrangements for the trip to Cheyenne. Tank was so grateful for Collin's social abilities.

"Can I go along?" Chip asked.

Alan nodded. "You just want to talk with the vets about caring for the bulls and such." Alan and Chip went off into a conversation of their own. Tank returned to eating as Collin and Maureen spoke about Collin's father and things back in England. Collin told her about what he knew was happening back home. Apparently he had spoken with one of the men on the estate. Tank knew he should be paying attention, but his mind seemed mired in long-ago things he needed to be able to leave behind.

"Sometimes our pasts have a way of sneaking up on us," George told him softly. "The only way to exorcise it is to get whatever it is out in the open. Then it doesn't have any more power over you."

"It isn't that," Tank said. "It's just that sometimes I don't know who I'm supposed to be."

Collin squeezed his hand. "You're supposed to be you."

"But what person is that?" Tank asked, and the conversation around the table screeched to a halt.

"Tank, honey, what do you mean?" Maureen asked.

Collin leaned forward. "I think Tank is still trying to figure out who he is." He met Tank's gaze with that gentleness that he knew he was falling for in his big blue eyes, so understanding and unjudgmental.

"How so?" Chip asked. "You're Tank. We know who you are. We grew up next door."

Tank shrugged. "I'm not that person any longer." Sometimes he felt like the floor under his feet was going to swallow him up. It was hard for most people to understand. "I'm not the kid you grew up with. The Army made very sure that person is gone. I spent years learning how to fight and being good at what I did. I fought side by side with men who thought nothing of doing what was necessary to win. I became one of them. And now I'm supposed to be that same guy I was before I left, and I can't do that."

"I know," Collin said softly. "I like the person you are now. You don't need to be anyone other than yourself."

This was very difficult, and it felt like he was about to rip his chest open for everyone to see. "But who the hell is that?" He spoke more loudly than he intended. "I came back, and then I threw myself into the ranch. I kept to myself and just worked because it was what I knew how to do and because it was safe. I felt safe." That took a lot to admit, and Tank couldn't take the scrutiny any longer.

"And what isn't safe now?" Collin asked.

Tank looked around the table, all eyes on him. He swallowed and stood, then thanked Maureen for dinner before getting the hell out of that room as quickly as he could. He went outside and around the corner of the ranch house, clenching his fists. "Fuck… fuck… fuck…," he hissed. Tank had seen battle, he'd fought for his country, and yet he couldn't face his own emotions. Those overwhelmed him and sent him running for the hills like a scared rabbit.

A hand pressed to the middle of his back. He turned to find Collin simply looking at him. "You know it's okay, big guy."

"No, it's not. No one understands."

"Then explain it to me." Collin leaned against the side of the building. "What has you so upset?"

"Because I'm not the soldier I was trained to be. I can't do that anymore. I'm not the kid I was before I left. That person is gone too. I've spent years trying to be a rancher, but all I ended up with is an empty house with only three dogs for company, and just when I thought things might be changing for me… it hits me that you're going to be leaving and I'm going to have to go back to being something I can't be again. Maybe that's my destiny. I'm stuck in a life that changes me, but then changes again, and I just can't keep up and will never fit in."

Collin blinked up at him, those huge eyes as beautiful as ever in the last of the evening light. "Did you ever think that the only place you don't fit in is right up here?" He placed his hand on the side of Tank's head. "Your men would follow you anywhere. They trust you, and come on… Denny walked in on the two of us having a good snog and didn't bat an eyelash. And as for the rest… our lives change all the time, and we all have to roll with it. No matter what."

Tank knew Collin was right, but it didn't make him feel any better. "I just want something more…."

"What is it you want, Tank?" Collin asked. "I'm not asking what you think you should do or what your family would have wanted you to do, but what is it *you* want?" He sighed. "Maybe I'm wrong, but it seems to me that you've been doing what you think you have to do." Collin went up on his toes. "But maybe it's time for you to think about what it is you want. Tank… what is it that's going to make you happy?"

With a question that no one had ever asked before, Collin slid his hand away from Tank's cheek. Then he turned and slowly walked back around the corner of the house. The back door slapped closed a few seconds later.

Tank blinked as he looked out over the rolling land. He knew how it behaved. This was where he had done part of his growing up; the land was part of him. But maybe it wasn't *all* of him. Collin's question was a simple one, and yet it was something Tank had never really considered. He'd gone into the service because it was a place where he knew he could get a good job and be able to send money home to help. Then, once he was out, he'd returned and taken over because somehow he thought he had to save the one thing his mother and father had tried to build, the one place he *thought* he felt at home. But even here, he was still a stranger of sorts. There was one thing—one *person*—who didn't make him feel like a stranger in a strange land, and that was Collin.

And like it or not, he would be leaving soon, and there was nothing Tank could do about it.

CHAPTER 12

"WE'RE GOING to be leaving in the morning," Tank was saying. "Just to Cheyenne for the rodeo."

Collin rolled over, burying his face next to Tank as he wondered if they ever slept in here. He yawned and roused himself out of sleep.

"Sure. Come on over. I'll make sure there's coffee." Tank hung up.

"What's going on?"

Tank pushed back the covers, and Collin pulled them back over himself. "The sheriff is coming out, and he wants to talk to both of us. It seems he has some information." His voice was as serious as a heart attack, so Collin got out of bed, checking the clock. It was a little after six. Granted, that was sleeping in for Tank.

"Did he say what it was?" Collin asked as he pulled on some pants and then a shirt. Tank had been super quiet since dinner at Maureen's last evening, but when they went to bed, Tank had held him so tight at times he thought he was going to squeeze the air out of him. Unlike previous nights, there hadn't been passion between them. Rather, Collin got the feeling it was a night of comfort. He did his best, but Collin wondered exactly what he was trying to comfort Tank for. The big guy had opened up to him a little, but something had really rocked Tank's core.

"No," Tank answered, pulling Collin out of his musings on the stunning man. He groaned softly to himself as Tank pulled on a shirt. He would very much have liked to figure out a way to entice him back to bed.

"I'll go get the coffee on and feed the pups. You can finish getting ready." If he stayed here for much longer, he was going to jump Tank, and he was pretty sure the sheriff would not appreciate walking in on that.

Collin got the coffee started and fed the dogs, finishing as the knock sounded on the back door. He let the sheriff in, and Tank joined them around the kitchen table.

"What have you got for us?" Tank asked as he poured mugs and set them down.

"Sullivan is going to be arraigned today, and I suspect his bail is going to be more than he can afford, considering we convinced the judge to freeze his accounts once we got access to them. It seems he received a sizable deposit from the UK about a week ago. We found where he got the cattle that were let loose on your land. He was hired to haul some sick cattle to the—"

"Knackers?" Collin supplied, and Sheriff Donaldson nodded.

"For disposal. It seems they were sloppy in their vaccination records and missed a few head." He sighed. "They hired Aaron Sullivan to haul them away, and it's those head that ended up in your field. We found the ear tags in his truck. He really isn't all that smart."

"So it seems my father is behind all this after all," Collin said, wondering what the hell he was going to do.

"Yes and no. The money came from the UK, but I don't know who sent it. I don't think Sullivan knows either. He says he was hired blind, and I think I believe him. The guy is scared half to death right now, and I think he'll say anything that he thinks will help him."

Collin nodded. "You know where the money came from, and he's told you what he was hired to do. That all leads us to my father. Who else in England would want to cause trouble here?"

"We have no direct proof," the sheriff said.

"I know. But there's enough that I may be able to get my father to provide it himself, especially if he thinks he's been successful." Collin's mind raced ahead. "My father is all about control. He wants to be the one to call the shots, and he hated that I took time away. He wants to be the one to control me and my life, including trying to get me to marry… a woman." He could see his father prowling through the rooms of the estate, scheming and stewing, trying to think of ways to ruin Collin's trip and make sure he came home and fell in line. Collin wasn't a puppet, but that's what the old man wanted. "My father's biggest fear is that I will discover some sort of life away from him and the family. Then there will be no one to do all the work so he can play lord of the manor and keep up his image as the earl. He has horses, but he hasn't ridden in years. It's all about this image of privilege that he has in his mind." Collin turned to Tank. "I really think my father is crazy. What sort of person hires someone to harass and put their son in danger while he's on vacation? That isn't reasonable."

"I can agree with that," Sheriff Donaldson said. "And I wish I could help you, but there is nothing I can do. My reach is only so far, and I have my hands full with the county here."

"Yes, but I'll give you the number for the local constabulary."

The sheriff sipped his coffee. "Will they be willing to act on it?"

"Oh yes. My father may be the earl, but he isn't well-liked. Father loves to look down on other people. It's his superpower, so to speak. Consequently, most people in the county aren't going to go out of their way for him."

"But that would also pave the way for you to take the reins." The sheriff was smart.

"If I'm honest, then yes, it would. But I want to make sure that the estate stays viable for the county and the people in the area. We're a source of employment and stability for people." Collin wasn't going to shy away from the truth. "I've known what my place was in the family and society and what my father expects of me since I was eight years old. That's when he officially conferred the title of viscount, mainly because my mother wished it. When he did that, he took me aside and told me what it meant. That I was his heir and that it was my job to take care of the estate, and ultimately have a son of my own to pass on the legacy." Collin cleared his throat. "There was never talk of love or care in my family, only duty and what was expected." Sheriff Donaldson's eyes widened, and Collin heard Tank's sharp intake of breath.

"How can that be true?"

"Part of the reason is because what he said was true. *Noblesse oblige*—with nobility comes obligation. What I didn't realize until I was much older was that my father thought my obligation was to him. That he could run every aspect of my life—and he tried, believe me. What I studied in school was chosen by him, and what I did when I was home was scheduled through him." Collin knew that neither of these two could understand what it was like living with his father. "So to make a long story short, when I decided to come here, that became a threat." He turned to look out the window at the open land that spread to the trees that rose at the northern edge. "The past ten days have been freeing, and I can breathe deeply, truly exhale, for the first time in my life… and I don't want it to end." He held Tank's hand tightly. "But I'm going to have to go back. I can't abandon everything and everyone back home. I was born into privilege, and because of that, I need to do what's right. But Sheriff, I'll tell you this. You can give me everything you now know, and that will determine whether I go back hobbled or with some strength. And once I'm back home, I can see if I can't put the pieces together and make sure my father gets what's coming to him." He turned to Tank. "I'm sorry for bringing all my family mess to your doorstep. That was not my intention."

"I know." Tank set down his mug of coffee. "And if a little drama is the price for you coming here, then it's a small one that I'd pay again."

The sheriff finished his mug. "I'll be off now, and I'll do what I can, I promise you that. Let me ask the judge if he'll approve me sharing what I have. I don't want to jeopardize the case we have here. That's the best I can do at this point."

"Of course." Collin stood and shook his hand. "I appreciate your help, and if there is anything more I can do, please let me know." He stayed standing until the sheriff left the house.

"We need to meet Alan and George at Maureen's. She said she'd have breakfast for us, and then we can go." Tank didn't stand, and as Collin passed behind his chair, he found himself caught in Tank's arms. "I meant what I said."

Collin smiled, his lips close to Tank's. "I know you did, and I know what it means." He did. The problem was that he felt the same way, and in the end it meant that Collin was going to be leaving with a shattered heart. But it was a small price to pay, and Collin would make the most of the time they had. It was his only choice.

"IS THIS the line to get in?" Collin asked as Alan pulled the truck to a stop. "This must really be popular."

"It will move pretty quickly, and yes, the rodeo is popular here," George said, turning to smile.

Collin leaned against Tank, excited to be there. Tank smiled indulgently at him, like he was a kid, and Collin was fine with that. He had learned that there were times when it was best to look at things through the eyes of a child. It made the world much more interesting than viewing everything as a cynical adult. "How long before it starts?"

"The first round was yesterday. I got tickets for today because it's the finals, so we should see some of the best rides. This is a two-day event, and it all winds up today. That's why there are so many cars." Alan pulled ahead, and they entered the arena and car park. They were directed to a space, and once Alan turned off the engine, Collin got out, stretching his legs. "Two hours doesn't seem like much to them," George said.

"I know. The only time I spend that much time in the car is when I have to drive to London or the beach." Collin worked his legs and fell in next to Tank, behind George and Alan.

"I'm going to take off to see the animals," Chip said and hurried away toward a side entrance.

"We might see him by the time the event is over," Alan explained as they continued inside and to their seats. George had arranged for really good seats down front so they could be right in the action.

"When does everything start?"

"In a little while," Tank told him. "Do you want something to drink or eat? I was going to get me a hot dog before things get started."

"Just something to drink." His belly was a little roily, and he wasn't sure food was a good idea just yet. Collin had never felt motion sick before, but being in the back of the truck seemed to get his belly going. "Thank you." He wasn't sure a show of affection was a good idea here, but he wished he could kiss Tank for his care and consideration. "Maybe I'll get something to eat later."

Tank headed off, and Collin watched the activity on the field as people rushed around, apparently getting things ready. Eventually everyone cleared out, and just about the time Tank returned, the announcer started his patter and announced the various competitors.

"Is this okay?" Tank asked, pressing a huge cup into his hand. Collin wondered what the heck it needed to be so big for, but he was learning that portions of just about everything were bigger here.

"Thank you," Collin said as he leaned forward to watch as the first event got under way.

Collin cheered and yelled through the events, having a great time and whooping it up until his throat ached. The energy in the arena seemed to edge upward with each event until Collin could barely sit still. God, this was so much fun.

"Do you want to meet some of the cowboys?" Alan asked before getting up and leading him down and around to the pens. He introduced Collin to friends of his and showed him around. Apparently he and Chip were well known in this circle, and Collin grinned from ear to ear at being included. After about an hour, they made their way back up to the stands in time for the final event, bull riding.

The stands were a mass of people cheering at the tops of their lungs as each rider pitted his skills and luck against the beasts'. Forget what anyone else said, these were modern gladiatorial games. Only hopefully no one would get injured and both man and beast would come out of the contest under their own power. One rider most definitely didn't, and the entire arena went quiet and held its collective breath until it was announced that he was going to be okay. Then the cheer went up just as loudly as it did for the announcement of the eventual winners.

It took a while to get out and down to the hotel. Collin was wrung out and as excited as he could ever remember being.

"What's this?" Tank asked as Collin kicked the hotel room door closed as soon as they were inside.

He raced to Tank, who caught him in strong arms. Collin wrapped his arms around Tank's neck and his legs around his waist before kissing him with everything he had. Sitting in those stands for hours had revved Collin up to the point where control was the last thing on his mind. He sucked on Tank's tongue, reveling in the taste of him and wanting more. Tank held him tightly, moving through the room until they reached the bed. Tank laid Collin on his back and leaned over him before plundering Collin's mouth.

When Tank tried to pull away, Collin pulled him back down. It wasn't until Tank tried to pull off Collin's shirt that he let go for just long enough to get his clothes off. Then Collin shimmied under Tank's body, radiating heat like a furnace. Damn, he loved the feel of Tank's skin against his.

"You're so… hot," Collin whispered. "Damned steamy."

"Is that good?" Tank asked.

Collin grinned as he gazed deeply into Tank's incredible eyes. "It's stunning." He held him closer, loving the heat and the slide of skin on skin. He was going to miss this, and Collin found himself taking note of the way Tank's hands slid under him and down his back, cupping his bum. He wanted to remember everything when he returned home. "*You're* stunning."

"I'm not," Tank countered.

Collin cradled Tank's cheeks in his hands, holding him still. "Yes, you are, and since I'm the one looking at you, it's my opinion that counts." He left off the *so there* and drew Tank back down into a deep kiss, patting Tank's side gently. He rolled them on the bed, and Collin grinned. "I like this position."

"You do, huh?" Tank said teasingly.

"Oh yeah. I like it when you're at my mercy." He sucked one of Tank's nipples, squeezing the other until Tank arched his back, groaning deeply. That was a sound Collin would never get tired of hearing. "Did you bring supplies?"

Tank's eyes widened. Clearly he hadn't thought of it, but Collin had. He dashed to the bathroom and spilled the contents of his kit on the counter until he found what he was looking for. When he returned, Tank had propped himself up against the headboard, legs spread, his hand slowly gliding up and down his ample cock. Collin climbed onto the bed and straddled Tank's lap, rocking his hips, Tank's cock sliding along his crease. "You seem surprised." He kept rocking as Tank gasped.

Collin opened the condom package and rolled it onto Tank. Then he slicked them both before slowly sinking down.

"Goddamn," Tank swore as Collin relaxed and sank deeper.

"You like that? Because I sure as hell do." Once he was seated, he stilled, closing his eyes and letting muscles that hadn't been stretched in a while relax. Then he began to move.

Damn, Tank was something else. He met each of Collin's movements with one of his own. Neither of them needed to say anything. This wasn't a time for conversation. Besides, Collin could tell when Tank's control was waning by the way his breathing grew shallower and more intense. Collin backed off and let Tank catch his breath before picking up the pace once more. Sweat broke out on Tank's forehead, and he held Collin's bum, trying to gain the control that Collin wasn't quite ready to give.

"Collin," Tank groaned, and Collin cut him off by slipping his fingers between Tank's lips. He sucked them, and Collin rode harder, his cock slapping his belly as he drove Tank to the point where his eyes crossed. Damn, Tank was so sexy. Collin stroked himself, clenching his muscles as Tank groaned loudly enough that he felt it rumble in his chest. That was damn near enough to send Collin over the edge. But he held on, riding Tank like the stallion he was.

"Save a horse, ride a cowboy," Collin teased, and Tank groaned again, this time for his bad joke, but the motion of his hips never stopped, and Collin met each of Tank's movements, loving every second, until a firm knock on the door threatened to pull him out of his passion haze.

"Just a minute!" Collin called, refusing to stop. He was so close, and Tank's shallow breathing told him that he was in the same situation.

The knock sounded again.

"I'm coming…," Collin cried as his release barreled into him, tossing him into the air like one of the bulls had done to his rider, except with this ride, he hung there for a good long time before landing firmly and carefully in Tank's arms.

"I feel like I just had the ride of my life," Tank said.

"It's good to know this English country boy can give the cowboys a run for their money." He patted Tank's chest and shivered when their bodies disconnected.

"Wasn't there someone at the door?"

Collin was about the slip under the covers when that knock came again, louder this time. He got off the bed, a beautiful soreness settling into his muscles. Tank hurried off to the bathroom, that beefy ass of his bouncing slightly with every step. Damn, that man was a sight—front or back didn't matter. He could raise Collin's temperature with just a look.

Collin pulled on his robe and peered through the peephole just as Chip raised his hand to knock again.

"Collin—"

Collin opened the door, making sure his robe was closed. "What's going on?" he asked more sharply than he intended.

"Alan and George sent me over. Your phone seems to be off…." He snickered at the massively rumpled bed. "But maybe not. You were just taking care of business."

Collin narrowed his gaze. "You're too old to be precocious, and you were interrupting."

"I know. But George got a call from someone back home. He said that they have been calling you, but no one is answering." Chip pulled off his hat and held it in front of him. "Apparently it's your father. George said that he's had a stroke and is in the hospital."

Collin stepped back, and Chip hurried inside.

"What?" Collin asked, and Chip repeated himself.

Collin fumbled on the floor next to the bed and found Tank's jeans. He slipped them into the bathroom before sitting on the edge of the bed. Tank came out wearing just the jeans.

"Chip, what else did George say?" Thank God Tank seemed to be able to think, because Collin's mind had stopped turning.

"Just that they found him in the house on the floor and that he's been taken to the hospital. George said to tell you that he is alive and that he's working to find out what he can. He said to come to his and Alan's room as soon as you are able." Chip looked at Tank and then at Collin before hurrying out of the room, closing the door behind him.

"Bloody hell and bollocks," Collin snapped as soon as the door closed. "That pain in the bum has to decide to have a damned stroke."

Tank put an arm around him. "It will be all right."

"No, it won't. He's nothing but a thief, and I refuse to let him decide what's going to happen in my life from the estate *or* from a hospital bed." He should have seen this coming. One way or another, his father got whatever the fuck he wanted.

Tank stood and began looking through the room before handing Collin his phone. It was dead. When he plugged it in and powered it up, he ignored the beeps of messages and calls. All he had wanted was two weeks to himself. Two weeks to try to figure some things out and maybe have a little fun.

He turned to Tank and felt his heart race. He knew his time here was abruptly coming to an end and that he was going to have to return home. He didn't have a choice. His father was right about one thing in his life: Collin had a duty to the family, the estate, and the people who worked there.

"We should go see what Alan and George have to say. Maybe they know more by now." Tank handed him his shirt, and Collin shrugged it on. He could already feel the chasm of thousands of miles and seven time zones opening between them.

"Yeah, I bet you're right." Collin pulled on his shoes as Tank finished getting dressed. When he was done, he sat on the edge of the bed once more.

"I know you don't want to go," Tank said softly.

Collin nodded. If he did—*when* he did—what he had with Tank would be over. Just like that. This little interlude would come crashing down around him, and that would be the end.

Finally, Collin gathered his strength and stood, left the room, and headed down the hall.

He knocked on the door, and George answered it and opened the door wide. Collin stepped inside with Tank behind him. Collin made for one of the chairs, but Tank slipped his arm around his waist, guided him to the end of the bed, and sat down, holding him without saying a word.

"Your father isn't conscious at the moment, but they say he's stable."

Collin nodded. "So what do we do now? I don't want to mess up everyone's fun." He was already thinking about how he could get to the airport and make his way home. George and Alan had a few more days with their family, and they shouldn't have to cut their visit short.

"Alan has been on the phone, and there are flights in the morning. Chip and Tank will drive the truck back, and the three of us will go on home to see to what needs to be done." Collin didn't have the will to challenge the authority in George's voice.

"I'm going with him," Tank said firmly. "Make arrangements for four." Collin was surprised and pleased at all the support, especially Tank's. And at least he had tested negative for anthrax, or else he wouldn't be able to travel.

"Five," Chip said.

Tank released him and stood in front of Chip. "I know you want to go, and I thank you for it, but we need you to drive the truck back for us, and I need you to look after things for me. Can you do that?" Chip nodded solemnly. "You can stay at my house if you like."

Chip might actually have smiled. "Thanks, Tank. I'll help you."

"I know you will."

"And later this summer, before classes start again, Alan and I will fly you over for a visit. We'll meet you in London, and you can see all the sights," George promised.

"Thank you, Chip," Collin said and pulled him into a hug. Back home that wasn't done, but here, it seemed like the right thing to do.

"No problem." He patted Collin on the back and then stepped away. "I'm going to go to bed because I'm going to have to do a lot of driving tomorrow. You all let me know if you need anything."

George followed Chip out into the hall, as Alan was still on the phone making arrangements, and Tank held Collin. For the moment, he felt safe. Tank did that for him.

"It's going to be all right."

"How?" Collin challenged. "Everything is going to change now. I have to take care of my father, and I'm going to be tied to everything back in England." He buried his face against Tank, inhaling that amazing scent, impressing it on his memory. "I'm going to have to see to it that the estate is run, do the job I was doing, as well as the one my father should have been."

Tank didn't move, those strong arms holding on. "It sounds to me like you got yourself a ranch to rebuild."

"I do."

CHAPTER 13

TANK SETTLED in his seat for their transcontinental flight. It had taken a while for them to reach Chicago, and then they'd had to wait almost six hours, but the four of them were on the plane. Tank didn't want to think how much these seats had cost. George had pulled some strings and called in a few favors. Apparently one of the men he went to boarding school with was a bigwig at the airline, and he had helped secure the business-class seats they were sitting in. "Try to relax and get some sleep," Tank told Collin, who was as wired as a high-voltage line.

"I can't."

"Are you worried about your father? We can call one more time before the plane takes off."

Collin shook his head. "I already called, and there's no change." He blinked a few times. "I know this is going to make me sound like the most selfish prig on earth, but I'm worried about the mess he's left me with." The cold in Collin's voice was almost enough to frost the windows.

Tank slipped his hand into Collin's as the plane backed away from the gate. He didn't say anything more because he really didn't understand the dynamic at play. It wasn't like he'd always gotten along with his father. Dad had been tough to get to know, and he tended to be a lot like Tank. His mother always said they were two peas in a pod. Still, he came to understand his father and that he had simply been overwhelmed and not able to keep up any longer. Life had picked up speed at a time when his father had been slowing down.

After takeoff, the flight attendants came through with drinks, and Collin ordered a couple glasses of wine, which he downed quickly. Once he ate, Collin reclined his seat as far as it would go and tried to sleep. Tank watched over him, worried about what was going on and relieved once Collin dozed off.

He did his best to let him sleep until they prepared for landing in London.

"Do you feel any better?" Tank asked as his third movie ended. If Collin had needed him, he'd wanted to be awake and ready.

Collin shook his head, looking out the window as their plane touched down.

George had made arrangements to get them home by train, and they shifted their luggage to the station in the airport. After a change at a huge London station, they were on their way north.

This time Tank drifted off. He'd spent too much time trying to stay awake.

"Tank," Collin said gently, "we're coming into the station."

Tank stretched and yawned, getting his muscles to work. Once they were off at the small local station, a man approached George, speaking very formally. He took their luggage to the Rolls.

"Should I take you home, sir?" the driver asked George.

"No. Collin needs to get to the hospital to check on his father. Please take us right there," George instructed.

Tank looked out the window at the flowing verdant countryside. It was all grass and trees of every shape and description. So different from the range back home. As they continued traveling, the open land gave way to a small city with homes right next to each other. It seemed to Tank that folks lived almost on top of one another.

Tank didn't try to figure out where they were going. There was no need. The driver knew, and Tank simply held Collin to try to comfort some of the building anxiety—which apparently only increased the closer they got, because by the time they pulled into the hospital drive, Collin's foot was bouncing on the floor. "We'll figure it out," Tank said softly. "You aren't alone. We'll be here for you."

Collin nodded but said nothing, getting out once the car pulled to a stop. He stood outside the building until the rest of them joined him. "I'm glad you're here."

Tank put his hand on Collin's back, just to let him know he was present. Then they went inside and were directed to a critical care unit. A nurse behind a desk told them, "I'm sorry, but this is family only."

Collin looked about ready to fall apart. Tank was unable to suppress a growl.

George patted his arm in an "I got this" way. "I'm sure you have your rules. The man in there is the Earl of Doddington. This is his son, the Viscount Haferton, and I'm the Duke of Northumberland. We're here to see the earl and help make sure both he and his son have everything they need." George flashed a smile, and Tank saw the moment the nurse nodded. Then he gave them the room number, and they went on down.

"Geez, that really worked."

George shrugged. "There are only a couple dozen dukes in the country. A good share of them are members of the royal family, so the title carries some weight." They stopped outside the room. "You and Tank go on in and see your father. Alan and I will be out here if you need us."

Tank followed Collin inside. The earl lay on the bed, his eyes closed, machines monitoring him, an IV in his arm. He looked peaceful, his chest rising and falling.

"Father, it's me," Collin said, but he got no reaction. Tank stayed back, letting Collin approach the bed. "I came back." The nearby machines displayed numbers and visualizations of his heartbeat, but other than their muted beeps, the room was quiet. Collin took his father's hand, sighing softly. Then he stood silently next to the bed for a few minutes before turning away. "I don't know what else to do."

"Sometimes people can hear what you say even though they aren't conscious. I heard that on TV." Tank knew he sounded lame. "Maybe tell him what you want to say in case this is the one chance you have."

Collin turned around. "What? I'm supposed tell him that he ignored me as much as he could while I was growing up and then tried to run my life for me?" He shook his head with another sigh. "That has to be the most un-British thing ever said." He turned back to his father. "You know, I could tell him that we caught the person that he hired to try to force me to come back. That I have evidence to turn over to the local constabulary, and that he could make headlines as the earl convicted of crimes and sent to prison. That should get the old bastard to wake up." There was so much hurt and anger in Collin. Tank wished he could help.

"Then tell him whatever you want to say. Good or bad. Have it out. Say what you want, and then maybe you can let it go." He patted Collin on the shoulder and left him alone, joining Alan and George.

They turned toward the room, probably expecting Collin to follow. Tank leaned against the wall.

"What's going on?" Alan asked.

"They have things that they need to say," Tank said.

"He's awake?" George asked.

Tank shook his head. "Sometimes it's just easier to get years of crap off your chest when the other person is comatose. Collin needs to clear the air with his dad." Tank settled in to wait.

After almost half an hour, Collin emerged from the room with a look of peace on his features that Tank hadn't seen before. His lips were relaxed, and his eyes held much less of the hurt that always seemed to be there before. "Any change?"

Collin shook his head. "We need to speak to the doctor."

"I checked while you were inside, and he'll be over soon." George went in to see Collin's father and emerged as the doctor strode up. They followed him inside, and the doctor closed the door.

"What's his prognosis?" Collin asked.

"Well, sir," he began, "his stroke was quite intense, but there is brain activity. We kept him sedated for a few days to give his system a chance to repair. We have backed off the medication, and hopefully he'll start to come around." Tank moved closer to Collin, just to be there. "But I'm afraid there will be lasting damage. We've run a number of scans, and this stroke is only the latest and most severe of the ones he's had over the past year."

"Excuse me," Collin said. "Others?"

"Yes. We believe he's been having small strokes for years. They probably went unreported, and he may not have known he was having them, but the earl has been in a state of mental decline for quite some time." The doctor was being professional, but his tone seemed almost detached. Maybe he had to be.

"I see. What do we do from here? There is business that will need to be managed, and so much to do." Tank could almost see a weight descending on Collin's shoulders, and he knew exactly what it felt like. Responsibility and duty could be damned heavy, nearly overwhelming. It didn't matter if you saw it coming. When it arrived, it could feel totally oppressive.

"Well, regardless of his physical recovery, it isn't likely that your father will be able to manage his own affairs. He is going to have some cognitive impairment. I'll put it in my report."

"Thank you," Collin said. "My father and I both thank you for all your help." He suddenly seemed very formal.

The doctor nodded respectfully and then left the room.

Collin turned back to his father, shaking his head. "We may as well go."

Tank followed them out of the hospital and back to the car. Tank sat in back next to Collin. "Let's get you home."

"Yes," Collin agreed, and they rode through the countryside while George made a few phone calls.

They drove up a long drive lined with trees and sprawling lawns to a large brick estate with multiple chimneys and white trim. The place looked solid, like it had seen the passing of many years and was ready to weather whatever lay ahead. They pulled to a stop in front of the door, and Tank climbed out and grabbed his and Collin's luggage before following everyone inside.

"Would anyone like a drink?" Collin asked.

Tank set the bags in the hall as the others went into a side room. Books littered one of the tables, even covering the seat of one of the chairs. Collin pointedly ignored the mess and sat on a sofa with his legs stretched out. "This is the family library. It used to be meticulously organized, but my father had a tendency to take a book and put it back anywhere he wanted, so over the years it's become a real mess. Just like everything else here." He sighed and grabbed a whisky bottle off a cart with some glasses. He held it up. Tank shook his head, as did Alan and George. Collin viewed the bottle before setting it back down again. "What in bloody hell do I do now?"

"Well," George said, "I'm assuming that your father didn't express his wishes as to what was supposed to happen if he became incapacitated."

"Unless we can find it in the rat's nest of his office, then your assumption is correct."

"What about his solicitor?" George asked.

Collin shrugged and seemed completely overwhelmed. Tank just wanted to get him upstairs to a bedroom so they could both sleep.

"Okay. I called mine to put him on alert. Let me send him a message. He can be here tomorrow and help you figure out the legal process. You're going to need to have some sort of authority to run the business here. Thomas can help you get all of that in order."

Collin simply nodded.

"I think I need to get him upstairs so he can rest." Tank didn't know what else to do. "Maybe after he wakes up, we can go back to the hospital?"

"No problem," Alan said. "Just call and I'll come pick you up and take you there." He stood. "Come on, George, let's let these two get some rest. I know you have calls to make, and I need to check on the tasks I left while we were gone." He guided George out, and Tank went to one of the deep-set windows, where he watched the two of them with a certain level of jealousy. Just watching them warmed his heart.

"Tank," Collin said, pulling him out of his thoughts.

They brought the luggage upstairs to a long hall that ran in both directions. "Which way is your room?"

Collin led him down to a large bedroom, neat and clean, with dark colors and heavy, rich furniture, incredibly masculine. Tank liked it a lot. The bed was large, with heavy wood and a thick comforter. He set down the luggage, and Collin went through to close the curtains. "The bathroom is right through there." He stopped. "There's another bedroom on the other side of the bathroom that you can use if you want." Tank scowled but didn't say anything. Hell, Collin suddenly seemed like he was going to shatter at any second.

"I'd rather stay with you." Tank took him in his arms. "Just go get yourself cleaned up and come back in here. I'm not going to leave you. I promise." He released Collin and watched him go into the bathroom. Once he was gone, Tank opened his hastily packed suitcase and got out his things. Once Collin returned, he took his chance in the bathroom and came back to find Collin already under the covers.

Tank undressed and slipped in next to him. He was bone weary, but more concerned about Collin than anything else. "If you don't want to talk, you don't have to."

Collin rolled over, pressing against him. "It's like my father had the stroke as the world's biggest up-your-bum. Like he can make me do what he wants one way or another."

Tank had no idea what to say to that. "Didn't you always know you'd have to take over?" Collin blinked before nodding. "Then it's coming sooner rather than later. And maybe that's a good thing. Your dad doesn't care about this place. That's pretty obvious." He cupped Collin's cheeks. "But you do. I see it in your eyes. You care a lot. So do what I did. Take over and manage the place the way it should be. Rebuild your own ranch and make it something you can be proud of. Talk to George and Alan. I know they'll help you."

"Yeah, I'm sure they will." He sighed. "But when Dad dies, I'm sure there's going to be a tax bill, and I won't have any way to pay it."

"Cross that bridge when you come to it." Tank smiled. "Alan told me that he and George have one of those estates that's open to the public. Maybe you could do that here."

Collin scoffed. "Not looking like this. Though I can contact National Heritage and see what the options are." He yawned, and Tank gathered Collin to him. "I need to rest."

"Then do that, and we'll figure out things when you're rested." Tank closed his eyes, willing himself to sleep, but his mind kept going to the fact that as much as he loved this—holding Collin in his arms and wanting him there all the time—this was just a temporary reprieve. He was here to help Collin get through a difficult stretch.

"Yeah. But I don't know where to start," Collin mumbled.

"We'll figure that out too. You and I will do it together." He smiled as Collin snuggled closer, and Tank slowly stroked up and down Collin's back until he fell to sleep. Tank just wished he could calm his own mind and follow him.

"THIS IS quite a place you have here," Tank said the following morning when Collin wandered into the huge kitchen area on the ground floor. Tank had explored the area once used by servants, as well as the main two floors and the old quarters on the third floor.

"Yeah, it is. A lot of the house is not used anymore. We have a lady from the area who comes in to clean, and there used to be a valet and butler who took care of things and managed the house, but he retired, and my father didn't replace him. Sometimes Tamsin will bring in a friend with her to do some extra cleaning." Collin sat down at a long table that had probably seen many servant meals around it at one point. "I see I'm going to have to get them."

"If I were you, I'd have a whole crew come in to tackle this area. It's really cool but needs a lot of work." Tank had enjoyed poking his head into spaces that hadn't been used in quite a while. "It's like a time capsule down here."

Collin took the offered cup of tea. "I'm sorry for yesterday," he said.

"There's no need to be. You needed to sleep, and I poked around a little. This place is like Downton Abbey, except not quite as big, but it has all that sort of stuff."

Collin nodded. "Walls filled with paintings that all need to be cleaned. There are rooms full of furniture that need attention. Rugs, ceilings, you name it. All of it will take money that I don't have." He finished his tea and seemed a little refreshed.

"It's all part of rebuilding the ranch," Tank said gently. "When does the solicitor get here?"

Collin checked the time. "A couple hours."

"Then why don't we try to tackle your father's office, see what's in there, and maybe we can get a sense of things. He's going to need to know anything we can tell him." Tank was thinking that if they could prove some sort of decreased capacity other than the say-so of the doctor, Collin might have a stronger case for taking over.

"Are you sure you want to go in there?" Collin swallowed hard.

"Let's do it. We can think of it as a treasure hunt." He grabbed the pot of tea, and Collin took the cups before they headed upstairs.

The office was a mess. Papers were piled everywhere, stacks on top of other stacks in some cases. "Where do we start?" Collin asked.

"I don't think it matters. Why don't we put any bills or things that are financial in nature in one place. Letters can go in another, and we can put junk mail in the trash." Tank found a stack of old shoeboxes sitting in the corner. They were empty, and he labeled each one and set them on the deep windowsill because it was the only clear space he could find. Then Tank cleared off a chair and started reviewing papers.

"It's pretty clear a lot of this is pure rubbish," Collin snapped an hour later as Tank took out a plastic trash bag and brought in another one. He opened it, and Collin added another stack of fliers and circulars.

"I found some things that I set aside." Tank had asked a number of questions about some papers and had separated out anything he thought might be meaningful, but he agreed that a lot of what was strewn around the room was trash. In an hour, the chair and sofa were clear, as were the nooks and crannies that paper had been stuffed into between books and under bric-a-brac, as Collin called it.

The financial shoebox was full, so Tank closed it and set another on top before walking over to the bookshelves. "What's in here?" Tank asked as Collin tackled the desk.

"I don't know. Those doors have been locked for years, and I don't think my father has the key," Collin said. Tank gently pulled on the doors below the bookshelves. They were indeed locked.

"Are there any old keys in the house somewhere?" Tank asked.

"Try the cupboard under the stairs in the basement. It's the one place I remember the old butler used to keep things like that." Tank left Collin sitting at the desk, sifting through more papers and shaking his head as he added more to the trash, while Tank found the door Collin referred to. He opened it to a board filled with keys. Some were on hooks that were marked, and others sat in a box on a shelf. Tank checked the hooks, grabbed the office keys as well as the unlabeled box, and returned to the office.

"I found all these, as well as keys to most every other room in the house," Tank reported. The keys on the pegs were to the office doors. He labeled them and set them on the table in the corner near the door. Then he began on the keys in the box, trying each of them in the various cabinets and glass doors in the room.

"Look," Tank said as one of the glass doors swung open to a cloud of dust. He closed it again, leaving the door unlocked, and labeled the key. "Maybe we're on the right track."

Tank continued working, door by door, key by key, releasing decades of dust and dirt. He sneezed and was about to hang it up, but he had about ten more to try. He found the ones to all the glass cabinets, but so far none of the keys had opened the doors under the bookcase. Tank picked up the pace, trying each of the keys, and with two left in the box, the key turned in the lock.

The front doorbell rang, and Collin started. Tank left the key where it was and went to answer it, then let in the solicitor, who was dressed in a suit. "Is the viscount available? Andrew Waddington."

"Collin is in the office. We've been trying to make sense of his father's papers. Mostly what we're finding are piles of junk." He shook the solicitor's hand and smiled.

"Maybe I can help," he said as Tank led him into the office. The solicitor introduced himself, and Tank got ready to leave. He figured this was family business.

"Just stay," Collin said, so Tank sat in one of the chairs out of the way. "What do we have?"

"I've looked into things since I talked to you and His Grace. I haven't been able to find any outstanding debts or mortgages. Your father has quite the reputation, but as far as I can tell, he didn't overextend himself."

"No. He just paid men to try to get me to come home from the only vacation I've ever had," Collin snapped, and told Andrew the story and what they had found. Andrew went through the records he had.

"It seems there was a withdrawal of two thousand pounds about ten days ago, and it was transferred to America." He frowned. "We can use that as grounds for diminished capacity, along with his current physical state and the recommendations of the doctors regarding his prognosis and medical history." He made notes. "Is there anything else you've been able to find?"

Collin pointed to the boxes. "Just mounds of financial-related papers and gobs of rubbish."

"Don't throw any of it out. Not yet. If you think it's rubbish, put it in storage until everything is sorted, just in case. As for the rest, I've filled out the basic paperwork for a conservancy for the estate. You'll be the logical choice since you are the heir to the title and everything else, so I don't anticipate any issues." He pulled out the papers and reviewed them with Collin. He and the solicitor signed them, and Tank acted as a witness.

"Is there anything I can't do?" Collin asked once Andrew got ready to leave.

"Once these are filed, I'll have copies sent over so you can take them to the bank and contact any organization you need so you can access the estate's accounts. It should take a few days. The biggest thing is that you are a conservator, which means you must do what is best for the estate and manage the money to the very best of your ability. Making major changes or selling major assets is something that would probably be frowned upon. But if you feel that is necessary, contact me and we can look into it." He shook hands with both of them before letting himself out.

"That went well," Tank said. "At least you know there isn't a mountain of debt somewhere."

"No. Just a ton of livestock, tenants, rents, and God knows what else to try to get my head around. I did a lot of work on the estate, but there were things that my father tended to either keep to himself or have others do, and I was too busy to try to oversee everything."

"I had to get myself up to speed when I took over from Dad. It took me a while to figure out a plan and strategy to get the ranch back in shape. You'll need to do the same things, and unfortunately that may mean selling the things that aren't producing. I had to slim down, because Dad loved to think of himself as a great horseman. Unfortunately what we ended up with was a barn full of livestock that had gotten older that we were just taking care of and not using. I sold a number of them for riding and other purposes. Then I was able to rent out stall space to bring in more income. It was a hard decision because they were Dad's."

"I know." Collin got comfortable behind the desk. Hell, he looked so good back there, like he belonged. "Dad has a string of ponies that he uses for the polo team he sponsors. It's an expensive hobby and one that I think is going to need to go. I figure I'll offer the horses to the players first and then sell them on the open market. Anything I get I'll put aside and use for the taxes on the estate trust."

Tank sat across from the desk. "And what will you do with the facilities and the people?"

"I don't know. I can lease the stable space. I have a few horses of my own, but...."

"The rest of the space can be put to use." Tank understood exactly what Collin was going through. The decisions he had made would not have gone down well with his father, but it meant the difference between a future on the land or selling up.

Collin set the page he was looking at aside. "I don't know what I'm going to do with anything yet. But we'll have to see." He picked up the papers again, and Tank went back to checking out the cabinets.

"What is this?" he asked, pulling out a gold-colored ship and setting it on the side of the desk.

"My God. I haven't seen that in years. My grandfather used to have grand dinner parties, and this would be in the center of the table. It's probably two hundred years old. My father must have put it away for safekeeping and forgotten about it." Collin pushed the chair out of the way, and Tank unlocked the other doors. They carefully pulled out the items from inside, with Collin shaking his head at each find. "I thought all these things had been sold or broken, but here they are." He almost seemed to smile.

"You remember them, then?" Tank asked, holding up a piece of glass that shimmered in the light coming through the window.

"This was one of my mother's favorites. She had it on her desk. I wonder why all of it was just put away." Collin looked over each item, and Tank saw him truly smile for the first time since they returned. He sat on the floor, holding these treasures, and seemed transported. Tank left him to his memories, wandering the rooms on the main floor once more. He ended up in the library with the box of unclaimed keys, wondering what else he might find.

CHAPTER 14

"COLLIN." TANK'S voice drifted in from the other room. Collin set the vase he was holding gently on the desk and got up, following the sound. "I found some more."

Collin entered the library and went over to where Tank stood at the far wall. "What is it?"

"I thought I was looking for more cupboards, but all the ones in here open and have more books in them. I'm assuming the ones inside are pretty rare. But look here." Tank ran his hand between two of the cases, then moved aside a bit of the decorative molding to reveal a keyhole.

"What the hell?" Collin asked as he stepped forward. "Did you find what opens it?"

Tank shook his head. "These keys are all too small." He set the box on the table.

"A bloody secret room," Collin said softly as he looked closely at the keyhole. "I doubt this key is in the box or hanging down on the pegboard. What I am willing to bet is that the key is in this room somewhere, hidden. My grandfather probably knew where it was, and my father might have, but neither of them are going to be telling us anything. It's even possible that the secret was lost before them."

Collin tried to think of what he knew about that room and came up blank. It wasn't like he had ever sat at his father's knee to listen to stories. His father was never like that. Collin tried to think of anything his grandfather might have told him, but nothing triggered a particular memory.

"Any ideas?" Tank asked.

Collin shook his head. "No. But I think we've done what we can do for today." He stretched his arms upward, and Tank pressed a warm hand to his belly when his shirt rode up.

"I agree. We need to get something to eat, and then maybe you can show me around... outside."

Collin nodded. "How about we kill two birds with one stone? There's a pub in town. We can eat there, and I can show you the estate. I suggest you get your riding things. The best way to do what we want is on the back of a horse." Damn, for the first time Collin felt like his future wasn't closing in on him. He had no idea why, but he was pretty sure it had everything to do with Tank.

"THESE ARE gorgeous animals," Tank said as noses poked out over the tops of the stalls, looking for treats and scratches. Tank handed out plenty of attention, and the horses seemed to gravitate toward him. Each of the grooms and stablemen acknowledged him silently.

"Most of these are for polo," Collin said as Tank continued speaking softly, meeting each horse. It was like he was being introduced to new friends.

"I see." They arrived at the end of the stables.

"This is Reginald Waterbottom," Collin said.

"You have to be kidding me. Who would name a horse that?" Tank asked.

Collin put his hands on his hips. "I was sixteen and thought it hilarious at the time. Reggie is great, and I even have a western saddle for you. Do you think you can get him ready?" Reggie was already nuzzling Tank's chest and getting scratches. If he were a dog, his back leg would be going a mile a minute. Collin got Jester brushed and saddled before meeting Tank in the yard. He had already mounted his horse and looked every bit the cowboy. Collin swallowed hard, unable to look away, because bloody hell, he was as stunning a sight as Collin had ever seen. "As you would say, you're going to have to beat them off with a stick."

"Come on," Tank said, rolling his eyes. "I'm getting hungry."

Collin mounted and walked his horse next to Tank's. "So am I, and it isn't for food." He gave Tank his best smoldering look before taking off down the drive and cutting his horse across one of the fields, with Tank right behind him.

"You're a sneak," Tank called.

Collin slowed his horse to a walk. "Maybe." He smirked as Tank caught up, and they rode side by side. "You can see the spire of the church in the village through the trees."

"Is the village part of the estate?" Tank asked.

"It used to be, and we still own a number of properties that we rent out, but most of the village is owned by the villagers themselves. George owns a few properties here as well. This is the very edge of the dukedom. Most of his property is off to the west of here." Collin continued pointing out highlights as they approached a road and continued on to a small square in the center of the village.

People were out doing their shopping, and more than one inquired about the earl. It seemed more out of obligation than real concern. Collin's father wasn't someone who liked to get to know people. Collin received a number of offers of help and support, though.

"They like you," Tank said as they approached the pub. Collin dismounted and noticed a number of people watching Tank with curiosity—and definite interest from a few young ladies. Tank smiled as Collin made some introductions before tying off the horses and leading Tank into the small country pub that was the center of village life.

The main room looked like something out of a movie, with dark wood and benches that were worn just enough to seem like the place had been there for generations. Which it had. This place hadn't changed in all the time Collin had been coming here, other than a few additional cricket flags on the walls and maybe some different beers behind the bar. Otherwise, it was solid, like coming home and knowing some things don't change.

"Do we sit anywhere?" Tank asked softly.

Collin motioned, and Tank took off his hat and sat at one of the tables near the front windows. Collin sat across from him. "Your hair is growing in," he said, noticing the dark fuzz. "Are you going to shave it or let it grow?"

"I don't know. Sometimes I think I shaved my head because it was easy, and then maybe I was doing it to intimidate people so they'd stay away." Tank ran his hand over his head, and Collin leaned over the table, his eyes widening. "What?"

"Don't do that. It's too damned sexy." He grinned, and Tank groaned. Collin noticed he shifted a little.

"What can I bring you gents?" Kitty asked. Collin knew her from when she was a tot playing in the back room of the pub while her mom worked out front.

"Why don't you bring us each one of your dad's specials and the best dark beer you have," Collin told her, but she wasn't paying attention—at least not to him.

"Are you a real cowboy? Like riding bulls and all?" Her eyes bulged a little.

"Yes, ma'am. Though I was never crazy enough to ride bulls. I herd cattle back home." He smiled at her, and Collin gritted his teeth but said nothing. It wasn't like Tank was going to be interested in her. He was just being nice. Still, Collin felt a rising pang of jealousy.

"There's a town social and dance tomorrow," she said, cocking her eyebrows as she arched her back. Collin stifled a snicker.

"That sounds like fun. Maybe if Collin's dad is feeling better, he and I will come." Tank winked. "What do you think, Collin? You want to cut a rug?" He winked again, and it took Kitty a second before the message sank in. Then she cleared her throat.

"Okay. Two specials and a couple dark pints." She hurried away.

"I hope you aren't mad," Tank said.

Collin grinned. "Are you kidding? You made your claim pretty forcefully." Just like he'd done back in Wyoming. His phone vibrated, and Collin excused himself and stepped outside to take the call. "Viscount Haferton," he said, not recognizing the number.

"Hello, this is Nurse Ellen Prater. I'm calling about your father." Her tone was gentle, and Collin's stomach clenched. "Your father is regaining consciousness. He's responding to voices and is beginning to move. He hasn't spoken yet, and his eyes are still closed, but his brain is registering additional activity."

"Thank you. That's good news. I'll be up as soon as I can." He returned inside and sat back down. "He's waking up."

"Then let's eat and we can go back and head up to see him." It seemed so reasonable and was the right thing to do, but for a few hours, Collin had actually been able to have a little fun. He should have known that as soon as he let go of some worry, something would happen. He needed to get used to this. Tank wouldn't be able to stay for very long, and then Collin would have to deal with his father, the estate, and God knows what else on his own. Not that he was going to complain about it to anyone. Collin knew he was expected to maintain a stiff upper lip, keep quiet, and somehow figure things out.

Kitty brought their plates of sausage, veg, and potatoes. Bangers and mash, an eternal favorite. Harmon, Kitty's father, always put in something special, and today it was garlic in the potatoes, which were amazing. "How is your father?" Harmon asked, coming out of the kitchen.

"We're on our way to see him once we're done here. He seems to be improving, but we have no idea what lasting effects there might be," Collin said honestly, knowing that all he needed to do was tell one person and the entire village would know the update in a matter of a few hours.

Harmon nodded and looked like he was going to say something, biting his lip slightly.

"You can say what you want," Tank said, speaking for Collin. "Straight talkin' is appreciated."

Harmon leaned closer. "Not to speak out of turn, but…." He paused and straightened back up.

Collin nodded. "I'm aware." Harmon's posture and demeanor spoke volumes. Collin knew that the village and most people in the area feared his father because he was unpredictable. Their lives often depended on what happened at the estate, and unpredictability made them nervous. "I'll do what I can."

Harmon nodded before returning to the kitchen. Collin finished his amazing lunch and his single beer. Then he paid the tab, and they returned to the horses and rode slowly back to the estate.

"I think I get it now," Tank said from next to him.

"What?"

"Just how much pressure you're under," Tank said softly. Sitting perfectly straight in the saddle, he was a sight to behold. "I thought I understood pressure and expectations, but I didn't have a clue. Everyone in that pub looks to you for something or other. They're worried about your father, but I think they're even more worried if he, for lack of better words, stays around."

Collin swallowed and nodded. "They are all hoping that I'll be able to come in and make their lives better somehow, but I don't know how to do that."

"Yes, you do," Tank said forcefully. "In fact, I'm willing to bet you already are, and that's why you're so well-liked and why they look to you. Whatever your father did to you or told you, he was full of shit." Above all else, he liked that when Tank spoke, it was straightforward and honest. "Look what you did with Barney and how he responded to you. That gift isn't just with horses. It's with people too." He pulled to a stop. "I had determined that I was going to live my life alone. I figured it was easier to do that than to try to figure out how to make a life for myself. I had the ranch and a few friends, and I thought that was enough." Tank turned away and started forward. "I was wrong, and you were the one to show me that. Fuck, Collin, you brought some light and life to me." He sighed. "Let's go."

Collin nudged Jester forward to catch up with Tank. "That was easy. Hell, *you* were easy. I could see so much of what you wanted because I wanted the same thing. I knew you were lonely, and hell, I was too. My life had been dictated by someone else, and for a few weeks, it wasn't. I was free, and you helped me feel that way." They continued forward, their horses knowing the way home. "But I don't know what's going to happen next."

"Well, you'll have to deal with your father, and you'll take all of this over. I'll go back to my ranch and try to figure out what to do next." He didn't turn to look at him, and Collin huffed under his breath.

"Is that what you want to do?" Collin asked.

Tank pulled his horse to a stop. "What choice do I have? My life is there, and yours is here. I couldn't ask you to leave all this and just walk away to come stay there with me. That isn't any more practical than me leaving my family's land to stay here. I know Alan did it, but he had family to step in. I don't have that."

Collin understood family legacy and duty. "Let me ask you something. Who are you doing it for? Who are you building the ranch for?"

Tank glared at him. "That's the pot calling the kettle black. Who are you doing all this for?" As soon as he asked the question, Tank looked back toward the spire of the village, and his shoulders slumped. "We both have obligations, so we can't just pick up and leave." He started back toward the house, and Collin rode along with him. Tank was right, and he knew it. There was very little either of them could do, and they had to make the best of it. Their cards had been dealt, and they both got crappy hands.

"WHO IS this?" his father asked when they walked into the hospital room. Even though his voice was soft, he sounded demanding, and Collin wanted to turn around and leave the pain in the ass to stew.

"A friend from America," Collin answered. The last thing he was going to allow was his father to get under his skin. "How are you doing?"

"I'm just great. My legs don't move well, and you can hear that I talk funny." His words were slurred, but Collin understood him. "I asked them when I can go home, and they won't give an answer."

"Because they don't know," Collin said. "You just woke up after a bad stroke." He didn't want to say anything, but it appeared his father's left side was most affected. His arm lay on the bed, and that side of his mouth drooped. "You need to rest and get better."

"What I need is to go home." He tried to sit up and failed.

"Don't be so damned stubborn. You need rest and healing." Collin let an edge steal into his voice. "Do what the doctors say." He held his father's icy gaze, refusing to back down.

"I have things I need to see to, and don't think you're going to push me aside while I'm sick." His voice grew softer as he became tired. "I'm more than capable of seeing to my own business."

Collin turned to Tank and then leaned close to his father. "You don't need to worry about anything like that." He wasn't going to lie to him, but he also wasn't going to get into this right now. He knew that if the situation were reversed, his father would not extend the same courtesy. "Just rest and get your strength back."

His father closed his eyes, and Collin grew quiet, holding Tank's hand.

"I don't know your friend. Is he new?" his father asked, and Collin answered him again. Then his father seemed to go to sleep, and Collin said a quiet goodbye before leaving the room.

"He's going to fight you all the way," Tank said softly as they walked to the elevator.

Collin said nothing until the doors slid closed behind them. "It doesn't matter. Everyone is counting on me, and I can't let them down. If he fights, then I turn everything over to the constables, and they can charge him with conspiracy and God knows what else. But as much as he thinks he can handle things, he can't, and it isn't likely he ever will again, regardless of how he fights." Collin was realizing that not only was the responsibility for the estate settling on him, but he was going to need to care for his father, most likely for the rest of his life. However he looked at it, his future seemed written for him, and there was nothing he could do about it, no matter how much the thought of going back to Wyoming with Tank appealed to him right now.

George and Alan had them over for a quiet dinner, which Collin was grateful for. He also appreciated that they didn't spend time asking about his father and what his next steps were. He did bring them up to date, and they agreed that he should continue moving forward with his plans. Someone needed to run things, and his father wasn't going to be able to do that in the short term.

"How much longer are you planning to stay?" Alan asked over bowls of pistachio ice cream.

Collin couldn't help setting down his spoon, the fatigue that had been building in him slipping away momentarily as he held his breath.

"Three or four days," Tank answered. "I need to get my flight scheduled soon. I have to get back to the ranch, but I don't want to leave Collin to face all this alone." He took a small bite. "Not that he can't…. And I know you all will help him…." Tank shook his head slightly and went quiet.

Alan patted Tank's shoulder. "Dude," he said gently, "you don't want to go because of what that means."

"Yeah," Tank said softly, and Collin swallowed hard around the lump in his throat. "But there's nothing I can do about it, and that sucks big-time." He finished his ice cream. "Would you excuse me?" he asked formally, and when George nodded, Tank pushed back the chair and left the small dining area in George's private rooms, his footsteps fading quickly.

Collin watched the other two. They had met and found a way to work things out. But Collin didn't see that for him and Tank. Alan had gotten lucky because his mother had stepped up to take over the family ranch. Alan had told him at one point that his mother had spent years grieving his father, but decided she had spent enough of her life missing him and needed to rejoin the living. Collin found that hard to picture. Maureen was a force of nature, and it was hard to see anything keeping her at bay. But maybe that was what finding someone had done for her, and now she was marrying again. There was nothing like that for Tank.

What was between him and Tank was destined to fade with time and distance. "I don't know what to do. I keep trying to see a path forward, but every time I look, it seems to dead-end with a huge tree in the way."

"I guess that sometimes there isn't a way forward."

"George," Alan scolded.

Alan shrugged as George continued. "There isn't and you know it. Collin is the future Earl of Doddington. And yes, he could go back to the ranch with Tank, but that would mean things here would fall apart and he'd inherit a disaster that he would need to deal with eventually." George patted Alan's hand. "*Noblesse oblige*. Letting that happen would affect everyone in the area, including some of the people here. He knows that everything is interconnected, just like it is back in Wyoming. One ranch's success brings more attention to the area, and that helps the others, just as one ranch's decline hurts everyone as well in one way or another. Collin can't walk away from things here any more than Tank can turn his back on his ranch. He has the same obligations Collin does."

"Yeah, I know. But—" Alan began.

George smiled gently at him. "You're a romantic at heart."

Collin turned away, suddenly feeling like he was intruding on a private moment. George was right. The only way they could be together was if one of them gave up everything. Collin couldn't do that, and he wouldn't ask Tank to either. It would only be a source of resentment that would never let up, and eventually it would poison what they had.

"Then what's the answer?" Alan asked, and Collin's attention returned to them.

"We make the most of the time we have," Collin said and excused himself. He suddenly needed to find Tank—*now*.

It took a little searching, but he knew he'd find Tank outside. He happened to be sitting on the terrace railing, looking out over the great lawn in the evening light. "Tank...." Collin sat down next to him. "Is company okay?"

Tank didn't smile. "You? Always," he answered.

"What are you thinking about?"

Tank sighed. "I keep wondering why no matter what, I keep coming back to things I can't have regardless of how much I want them. I have to go back and—"

"Yet this is the most beautiful place you've ever seen and you don't want to leave it," he teased, but Tank turned to him, completely serious.

"I don't want to leave you," he clarified, and Collin's attempt at humor faded. Tank tugged Collin against his side, and they sat quietly together as the light dimmed. Alan and George joined them after a little while, and the four of them watched the sun set until an evening chill forced them inside. Collin thanked George and Alan for dinner and drove Tank and himself back home.

Once inside the house, Collin excused himself for a few minutes and made a call to the hospital. They told him that his father was resting and that he was still very weak and had been speaking a little at times. Collin hung up and found Tank in the library, looking at the books on the shelves.

Collin was worn out, but when Tank turned around, his gaze grew heated. He smiled and then drew closer before taking Collin's hand and leading him through the house and up the stairs, turning out the lights as they went. At the door to Collin's room, Tank guided Collin inside, then closed the door with his foot before pressing Collin against the bed.

Tank didn't say anything; he didn't need to. The earnest energy in his hands and the way he tugged off Collin's shirt and held him like he couldn't bear to have an inch of space between them said it all. His hands shook a little as they moved over Collin's body.

In the darkness, Collin took the opportunity to map the contours of Tank's back and sides with his hands, committing to memory the movement of each muscle. They were going to have to part, Collin knew that, and he was determined to remember everything possible. Tank kissed his breath away, and Collin quivered under him, breathing deeply when Tank pulled back.

Collin could only see Tank's outline, but that was enough. The intensity of his gaze seemed to make itself known, and he didn't dare look away. Even in the dark, he wanted as much as he could get. Collin stroked Tank's cheek, leading him back down and into a kiss.

They rolled on the bed, back and forth, each desperate for the other. When Collin was on top, he stroked Tank's chest, loving the coarse roughness of the hair against his fingers. He managed to get the waist of Tank's pants open before Tank rolled them and he was on the bottom, Tank's weight pressing him into the mattress, solid and firm. It made him feel safe, and Collin ran his hands down Tank's back and under his jeans, clasping his firm backside as he pushed the fabric lower. He wanted to feel all of Tank.

Tank must have understood, because he climbed off the bed. Twin thunks followed by the clink of his belt on the floor told Collin that Tank had shed his shoes and pants. Strong fingers tugged at Collin's shoes until they joined Tank's, followed by his trousers, until he was bare. Then Tank climbed back onto the bed, the heat between them growing. Still, Tank remained silent. His hands said everything that was needed. It was almost sublime, how much the silence in the room added to the intensity between them. Words were superfluous, and they had a much better use for their lips and mouths than talking.

Collin couldn't get enough of Tank—the feel of his hands, the contours of his skin under Collin's fingers, the taste of him that burst on his tongue. It was almost too much, and yet Collin wanted more. He pressed upward, and Tank sat back and held him as Collin repositioned himself until his legs wrapped around Tank's waist and he held him even tighter, like Tank was afraid Collin was going to get away.

Things grew more heated. The very air in the room seemed charged with electricity. Collin found a foil square on the nightstand and pressed it into Tank's hand. Tank set it aside and cupped Collin's cheeks in his hands. "I want you too," he whispered, drying Collin's throat to the point he could only nod.

Tank held him close and positioned Collin on his back before drawing closer. Then he paused and fumbled on the table next to the bed. Collin closed his eyes. A soft snick sounded like a gunshot in the silence, and then Collin gasped as slick fingers teased the sensitive skin around his entrance. He held his breath, but Tank soothed him, running those long, thick fingers over him, up and down, gliding over him until Collin could barely breathe. Each motion made him want more, and yet Tank seemed intent on driving him crazy.

Collin writhed on the bed until Tank slicked his fingers once more before entering him. He gasped and sighed as Tank made his vision double. He wound his arms around Tank's neck, kissing him as he sank that digit deeper, then scissored in a second finger.

"Tank," Collin whispered, breathing his name like it was the most important sound he had ever made.

Tank pulled away, and Collin gasped as Tank sank into him. Their joining was intense. Collin held the bedding in his fists as Tank ramped up his intensity. Collin could feel Tank losing control. Hell, Collin barely had any of his own, and rather than holding on, he let go and gave himself over to Tank, who only intensified his movements.

The bed began to rock, and Collin found himself mumbling incoherent sounds, but it was all he could manage. "Don't stop."

Tank caressed Collin's belly before taking his length in hand, stroking Collin to the timing of his hips. It was amazing. Collin held on to Tank, afraid he was going to fly into a million pieces at any second.

"I'm not going to." Tank leaned forward to kiss him as sweat broke out all over Collin. His entire body seemed to belong to someone else, because he had never been so complete. It was like he could feel what Tank felt and understand what Tank was thinking. He cupped his cheeks as though that would allow him to have a better connection. "You're mine, Collin," Tank whispered, and then thrust hard before stilling. Collin felt Tank fill the condom, and it shattered the last of his control. Collin tumbled into a mind-blowing release that left him floating for what seemed like hours.

Collin came back to himself slowly with Tank still holding him. He kissed him, shaking as their bodies separated. He sighed softly, settling back on the mattress while Tank took care of things in the bathroom and then rejoined him in bed.

"Did you mean what you said?" Collin asked.

Tank held him closer, pressing his chest to Collin's back. "I always mean what I say. A part of you will always be mine, just like you will always carry part of me, no matter where we go or how far apart we are." He kissed Collin's shoulder. "The ones we love are always with us, and I do love you."

"I know, and I love you too," Collin said as he put a hand on top of Tank's, then shifted closer, letting warmth surround him, and tried to go to sleep. He was well aware of the fact that sometimes love just wasn't enough. No matter what, he was in for some very cold and lonely days once Tank went home and took the warmth along with him.

CHAPTER 15

FOR THE next few days, they went to the hospital to visit Collin's father each morning. He seemed to be making progress, but he was still confused, stubborn, and forgetful. The earl's mobility had improved somewhat, but he was still in fragile health. In the afternoons, Tank went with Collin on estate business, checking on each of the operations and making sure all was in order. He worked with the estate's sheep man as well as the stable master, rolling up his sleeves and helping out where he could. It felt good to get his hands dirty.

"We're going to miss you," one of the boys said as Tank finished up in the stable for the day and pulled on his jacket.

Tank smiled and nodded. He had done his best to fit in, and he knew the easiest way to earn the respect of a man who worked for a living was to spend a day right alongside him. "I'm going to miss all of you too."

Tank walked slowly down the row of stalls, greeting each of the horses as he went. "I'll miss them as well." He said a final goodbye to each person he met, shook their hand, and wished them each the best. Then he let one of the men drive him back to the house, where he took off his boots and went inside.

"Tank?" Collin said as he came out of the library. "Done for the day?"

"Yes. I need to clean up and pack. My train to London leaves first thing in the morning."

Collin set aside the papers he was holding. "You know you can't leave. We never figured out how to get into that secret room." He put his hands on his hips. "And you can't leave until we do." Collin tried to hold a straight face, but he failed.

"Is that so? Then by that logic, we should never look for the key, and then I can't go away." God, that idea sounded enticing. "But I have to, and you have so many things to do here. You don't need a cowboy getting in your way." His throat ached, and he needed some distance or else he was going to break down in tears. Tank left the room and went upstairs, grabbed clean clothes, and went into the bathroom. It was old-fashioned but had a decent if tricky shower. Tank stripped down and got under the water, then washed up quickly before shutting it off. He pushed the curtain aside to see Collin standing outside, glaring at him like he was in for a gunfight.

"Do you really think you'd be in the way if you stayed?" Collin seemed to have a good head of steam.

Tank scratched the back of his neck. "Do you really think you can introduce me to your friends? I'm rough, and I make my living outdoors. We had a nice time at George and Alan's, but I saw all that finery all over. The dining room in this house looks like the king could come to visit at any time. And what if someone like that does decide to come calling?" He shook his head.

Collin closed the distance between them. "This is some excuse to make leaving easier. I know it."

Tank nodded. "Maybe it is. But who can blame me? Or you? I have to go, and you need to stay." He sighed. "After meeting you, things in my life are never going to be the same. For years I was fine being alone." He was never going to be able to go back to that, because now he knew how his life could be if he shared it with someone. The problem was that the one person he wanted, he just couldn't have. Tank took Collin into his arms, held him, and said nothing. Sometimes words weren't enough.

Slowly Collin wound his arms around Tank's back. "I don't want you to leave either. But I understand. You have to go the same as I had to return here."

There was nothing more to say. Tank lifted Collin off his feet and carried him toward the bedroom. He had to leave in the morning, but he was damn well going to give them both a memory to hold on to.

MORNING CAME way too early. Tank blinked at the clock beside the bed and got up. He dressed, took his bags downstairs, and left them near the front door. Collin came down just as George and Alan arrived. "You didn't need to come," Tank said before Alan hugged him. Then George did the same.

"We had to say goodbye," George said.

Alan nodded. "You take care, and tell Mom and Chip that I will see them for Mom's wedding in a few months." He half smiled. "You take care of yourself." He stepped back and nodded. Then he and George said a final goodbye before leaving.

Tank loaded his bags into Collin's car, and once everything was inside, Tank got in, and Collin pulled out and maneuvered the car down the drive. Tank turned to look at the house a final time before looking forward. He refused to break down and held his head high all the way to the train station. Once they arrived, Tank got out and got his bags, then stood next to the car. "I don't know what to say," he whispered.

Collin nodded, his eyes puffy and his lips trembling a little. Tank hugged him tightly.

"Take care of yourself, and for goodness' sake, spend some time with your friends and give Sheba and the pups some treats for me." He backed away, and Tank picked up his bags and headed for the train. He told himself he wasn't going to look back but did anyway, just before entering the station. Collin raised his hand and forced a half-smile.

Tank was so tempted to drop his bags and hurry back to him, but he nodded and smiled before turning into the station waiting area. His head ached, and his heart felt like it had been ripped from his chest, but he tried to ignore all of it. If he was numb, he wouldn't have to feel it, and he could try to go home and get on with his life.

Tank could tell himself that as much as he wanted, but it was easier said than done.

A FEW hours on the train was nothing compared to the bustle of the huge London airport and then mind-numbing hours on flights back to the States. Tank tried to rest but ended up running over his visit with Collin again and again. Their rides across the fields and woods, working with the beautiful horses in Collin's stable, talking with the man who managed Collin's sheep, afternoons in the pub for a pint. Even the visits to see Collin's cantankerous father in the hospital. It had all seemed so ideal and maybe a little unreal. He snorted as he looked out the airplane window, the reality of the time he'd had with Collin already fading into something as ethereal and hard to grasp as the clouds below them.

"Would you like something to drink?" the flight attendant asked.

"A beer, please," Tank answered, trying to rustle up a smile and failing. He stared out as the plane headed west, taking him farther from Collin with each passing second, and there was nothing he could do about it. Nothing at all.

IT TOOK an additional flight and hours' more travel, as well as a ride from Chip, before he stood outside his home once more. Apparently Maureen had brought Sheba, Liza, and Danny home from her house, because they were waiting excitedly for him, tumbling over each other for his attention. Tank put his bags down and knelt, then picked up each of them for kisses and plenty of attention. The pups had grown, and all three dogs seemed happy to see him, which warmed his heart.

"How about some treats?" Tank said as he stood up and opened the cupboard to give a Milk-Bone to each of the dogs, who hurried off to protect their treasure from the others. Tank put his bags in his room, looking down at the tidy bed where he and Collin had made love. He shook his head before closing the door behind him, then trudging through the house and out to the barn, where the horses all looked out to greet him.

Tank greeted each one, using caution around Barney, who seemed to be looking for Collin. Tank gently patted his neck and gave him a carrot before moving on as he wondered if there was any place on his own damned ranch that wouldn't remind him of Collin.

"Boss, you're back," Denny said before setting down a bale of hay to portion out to each horse. "Did you have a good trip?"

"I did. How are things here?"

Denny gave him a rundown of where everything stood. "We had a hard rain while you were gone. The storm came out of nowhere. There was some damage, but I got it repaired already, though you might want to get some more stone for the drive."

"Good deal," he said, smiling. "What else is going on?"

"Not much. Just that Maureen sent out wedding invitations. I'm sure there's one for you in the mail I put on the kitchen table." He nervously scratched the back of his neck. "I gotta ask, are you going to go back?" He shifted his weight from foot to foot.

"Where?"

"Back to England to be with Collin," he clarified. "Or is he going to come here?"

There must have been plenty of speculation going on. "You know one of those estates like they have on *Downton Abbey*?" Not that he had watched it, but everyone knew about it. Denny nodded.

"My wife watched it."

Tank huffed. "Well, Collin has one of those back home, and George has an even bigger one. They take a lot of work, and there's a ton of family business and drama wrapped up in them. So Collin isn't going to be coming here. And I have this ranch, and, well, I can't just pick it up and move the whole thing to England." He really didn't want to talk about this. "What do we have to do today?" It was best to get the conversation on work. Fortunately Denny took the hint and shifted the topic to the tasks left. Tank got busy, hoping that maybe physical activity would clear out some of the cobwebs and help him get his head on straight.

MAUREEN SET a dinner plate down in front of him. He thanked her and did his best to listen to the conversation, which was all about the wedding in a few weeks. Claude sat in the chair near hers, and the two of them looked like school kids, the way they grinned at each other.

"Have you heard from Collin? Do you know if he's coming with Alan and George?" Chip asked.

Tank shrugged. "I talked to him a few days ago. He is really busy putting things in order. He said his father's health is improving a little, but he doesn't know if he can get away." Each conversation with Collin seemed more and more remote. Maybe that was just the way of things. They hadn't seen each other in over a month. He and Collin had only been together for a few days, so maybe it was natural for things to cool.

"Tank, honey," Maureen said, pulling his head out of the clouds and back down to earth.

"I'm sorry," he said and tried to pay attention to what everyone was saying, but his heart just wasn't in it. His head was thousands of miles away. He found himself doing the time-zone match in his head, wondering where Collin was and what he might be doing at the moment more times a day than he could count.

Tank finished his dinner and waited until the others were done before thanking Maureen for the invitation.

"You're welcome. Go on in the living room. I'll be there in a minute," she told him, and Tank did as she asked, standing near the side of the sofa closest to the door until Maureen came in alone. "You need to do something," she told him seriously as she sat in her chair. "It's been weeks, and you still look like someone kicked your dog." She took his hand.

"What can I do? He's over there taking care of his father and that estate of his." He wasn't going to say it, but he was a bit intimidated by all of it. "I can't fit in over there, and Collin needs someone who can help him in that life. Besides, I have the ranch here, and I can't just walk away from it. This is my home just as much as Collin's is over there."

She nodded. "I know, but you got to do something. You can't mope around for the rest of your life. You get up, go to work all day, make something to eat, and then fall into bed, only to do it all over again the next day. You're trying to run away while standing still at the same time, and it isn't going to work."

"What am I supposed to do? I can't have what I want, so I do what I can. I work and hope that things will feel better. They say that each day it's supposed to get easier, but that's bullshit. Pardon my language," Tank said.

Maureen rolled her eyes. "You're supposed to get on with things. Find someone to share your life with." She sounded so reasonable, but the idea of going out with anyone other than Collin made his stomach roil.

"I can't just go out with anyone else. That would be wrong," he said before he could stop it.

Maureen nodded slowly. "Because you're in love with him. This isn't some infatuation or passing thing. You fell in love with him just as I suspect he did with you." She pointed to the seat, and Tank plonked himself down. "This is a bit of a pickle."

"It's impossible, that's what it is, and I have to accept it and try to get over it." That was the only option. "So please just let me do it in my own way."

Maureen shook her head. "Okay, I will, but don't expect me to sit around forever and just let you pine away." Dang, she was something else.

"What are you going to do?" Tank asked. Not that there was an answer. "And before you even think about it, don't go setting me up on blind dates or something."

She laughed, sitting back in the chair. "That's the last thing I'd try. Young man, you have your heart set on one thing, and maybe if you're lucky, you'll get it somehow."

Tank sighed, leaning forward and resting his head in his hands. "I don't see it."

She stroked the top of his head. "Love and life work in mysterious ways." When he looked up at her, she still had a smile that made him wonder what she was thinking. "By the way, I like your hair. Letting it grow out makes you look softer and really handsome."

"I started growing it out when I was gone. Collin said he liked it too." Why did everything lead back to him? "I think I should go on home. Thank you for the dinner. I appreciate it very much, even if I'm terrible company." He stood and turned to leave, but Maureen took his arm. When he looked at her, she gave him a hug.

"I'm a mother, and just because my kids are grown doesn't mean I can turn that off."

Tank held her gently in return. "But you aren't *my* mother."

"Details, details," she said, giving him a squeeze before backing away. "You have a good evening."

Tank nodded and left. He intended to go home, but instead he got into his truck and turned in the other direction and just drove. There were times when being out on the road, away from everything, allowed him to think. Eventually he pulled off to the side, got out, and lowered the tailgate. He sat on it and watched the sun set, then lay down as the stars came out. He wondered if Collin could be looking at the same stars that he was.

God, he had turned into such a sap. He had work to do, and yet he couldn't help lying here, wondering about Collin.

"I wish you were here with me," he admitted out loud. "I miss you." He sent the words out into the night, and then, after watching the constellations for a while, got back in the truck and went home.

As usual, Sheba was happy to see him. He passed out treats and then got ready for bed, grateful when all three dogs joined him in the now empty-seeming bed. Tank rolled onto his side, facing the unoccupied other half of the bed. He now clearly understood the difference between being alone and being lonely. For years he had lived on this ranch alone and never given it a second thought. But now he was tooth-achingly lonely and had no fucking idea what to do about it.

CHAPTER 16

COLLIN HELPED his father from the car into the house. He refused to use his walker, which meant that Collin needed to hold his arm the entire way. "I want to go to my office," his father snapped as soon as they stepped inside. Collin tried to steer him to the sitting room, but his father was having none of it.

"Okay. Let me help you." Collin opencd the door and let his father slowly make his way inside.

"What did you do?" he snapped, looking around the now organized and clean room. "Where are all my papers?"

Collin helped him to the nearest chair. "If you mean the stacks of newspapers and marketing trash, it's been gone through and discarded. But if you're referring to the bills and financial statements, they've been filed, paid, and the accounts brought up to date." He kept his voice level. "It's all in the desk files where you can look them over." He had put the treasure he and Tank had found back in the cabinets for safekeeping... for now.

His father wagged his finger at him. "I don't know what you're up to, boy, but I'm still the earl, and this is my office and I will do things the way I want. You can go, and I'll make sure that everything is put right." He hefted himself up and shuffled over to the desk. "Where are the log and checkbook?"

Collin leaned over and opened the top drawer. "Right here."

His father pulled them out and leaned forward to read the print. The stroke had affected his sight to a greater degree than he was willing to admit. Collin sighed and pulled up a chair across the desk.

"How did all these get paid? Who has been signing my name?" He slammed the book on the desk, glaring at Collin. "If you've done anything, so help me, I'll...."

"What?" Collin asked firmly. "You will do nothing. Someone has to see to it that things are managed properly, and I have a court-approved power of attorney. You have been in the hospital with a stroke, so I have taken on the management of the estate myself."

"Well, I'm back now, so you can leave me alone." He opened the ledger and started reading.

Collin had been putting off this conversation and had been trying to avoid it for weeks, but it was impossible now. More than anything, he wished he had Tank here to back him up. Not that he would be able to convince his father of anything. It was just that the support would be nice. But Collin had to stand on his own two feet, alone.

"Actually, I can't. I have been granted authority to conduct the estate business, and it's going to stay that way. You haven't been taking care of things for a long time, and it's taken weeks to get everything in order. All of the rents have been collected, and all expenses have been paid. At the moment, the estate coffers are nearly empty, but we're current and all debts are paid." He leaned over the desk. "However, with your stroke and the fact that your memory and cognitive abilities have been affected, it's best if I continue to manage things."

"I do not agree!" His father slammed his fist on the desk. The doctors had told him to stay calm, but as usual his father never paid attention to anyone other than himself.

"Then I'll contact Scotland Yard, as well as the local police, and they can arrest you." Collin kept his voice even. "You see, the man you hired in America to try to scare me into coming home because you wanted me under your thumb has been caught. You did a very bad job of hiding your tracks, and the funds transfer has been traced back here. It isn't going to take much for the local constabulary to trace those funds from your accounts."

His father glared at him.

"Those details were shared with the judge when I requested power of attorney, and he agreed that international crimes were not the behavior of a person in charge of their own faculties, so for the moment, he hasn't brought charges." Collin paused and let the implications sink into his father's now much slower mind.

"You little shit." His father sat back in the chair. He might have been angry, but Collin could see the fatigue in his eyes.

"No, Father. You did this, I didn't. It's your behavior that brought this on." At the moment, Collin felt surprisingly little for his father, and it was shocking to him—probably one of the saddest moments of his life.

"I'm in charge of the running of the estate for the workers and for the future. You will still be the earl and no one will be any the wiser. I will run the estate and family business, with your help if you wish. But from now on, all final decisions are mine. It is not my intention to humiliate you, and I won't."

"As long as I behave?" he supplied.

Collin searched for the right words. "You'll have time to enjoy yourself and not have to worry about this place, flocks, and everything else. Next week is the big cricket tournament between our village and the duke's. You'll be out there to captain our team the way you always have. Very little is going to change." Except that now, for good or bad, the decisions would be Collin's to make and live with. Collin could almost feel the final weight of responsibility settling on his shoulders, and it was heavy indeed.

"I see." His father sat a little straighter in the chair. "So I don't have to worry about this any longer. It's all your responsibility now."

Collin nodded. "Exactly."

His father got up from the desk, and Collin got him the walker. "Take me to the lounge. I think I want to watch the telly."

"I can bring you a book if you like," Collin said. "I got some of your favorites in big print editions so they will be easier to read. I can bring those to you." His father nodded, and Collin walked with him down the hall and got him seated in one of the overstuffed chairs. He brought in the books and made sure his father had the remote before going upstairs to his rooms.

Collin lowered himself into the chair in his room and checked the time before sending a message to Tank. His phone rang a minute later. "How did it go?"

"I'm not sure. I told my father how things were, and I expected him to fight me. He did at first, but then he just capitulated," Collin told him. "I wonder what the hell that means." His father was always one of those people who, when he encountered a roadblock, tried to go around it any way he could. A full attack on all fronts.

"Maybe he's thinking about what he'll do next," Tank offered. Though there wasn't much he *could* do. Collin and the legal system had pretty much boxed the old man in. "Or maybe he's just tired of fighting."

Collin sighed. "That could be it," he whispered. "He and I have been at odds for so long."

"Dad told me at the end that he understood what was truly important. That the chatter and petty things fell away. Maybe that's what's happening."

Collin would like to think so, but he wasn't going to let his guard down. God, being on guard like this was not the way he wanted to live. Hell, rambling through this big house alone was not how he wanted things either.

Collin had hoped that talking to Tank would make things easier, but all it did was clarify how much he missed him. "Ummm...," he started before cutting himself off. Those vocalizations had been trained out of him years ago, and he self-corrected quickly. "How are you doing? I got the invitation to Maureen's wedding. It was so kind of her to include me."

"Are you coming?" Tank asked, tellingly quickly, and Collin smiled. At least he knew Tank missed him as much as Collin wished he could be there.

"I don't know, but I doubt it. I have to stay here with my father. He can't travel, and I can't leave him here alone for days or a week." He had thought about ways that he could go ever since the envelope came in the post weeks ago. Wyoming was quite a distance for him to travel now. Collin closed his eyes and wished things were better. So many times, he had wondered what it would be like if he were in charge of things instead of his father, and now he got the full picture. It meant responsibility and putting the estate and the needs of the people on it before what he wanted. Fuck, even his father had to come first. Damn it all.

"I hope you can figure out a way to attend." The longing in Tank's voice sailed through the phone and right to Collin's aching heart. He wanted to tell him that he'd move heaven and earth to be there just so he could have a few precious days riding with Tank and sleeping in his arms. When he closed his eyes, Tank's voice in his ear, he could almost feel his work-rough hands on his skin. He released a soft sigh, and Tank growled, making Collin ache a little more. Fuck, he wanted to hear that again.

Collin blinked and swallowed hard, the momentary illusion popping like a soap bubble. "How are the dogs? Is Barney improving?"

He needed to change the subject immediately or else he was going to lose control and try to fuck his damned phone.

Tank chuckled. "Don't think I don't know what you're doing." That growl was back, deeper and more intense.

"Where are you?" Hell, he was almost shaking.

"In the barn," Tank answered, his voice deep.

"Okay, then, Mr. Hot-and-Growly, take a deep breath because we cannot have mobile sex right now, and you know it."

Tank huffed. "Fine. Barney is missing you. I give him treats, and he's letting me work with him. But I swear every time I come into the barn, he looks to see if you're with me. Sheba is doing well. The pups are growing and getting bigger, though sometimes it's hard to tell. All of them have taken to sleeping with me at night. They help fill that big bed."

And just like that, Collin was right back there in that bed, with the windows open, the night sounds filling the room as Tank filled him, moving nice and slow, drawing out the pleasure until Collin wanted to scream. He was tempted to undo his trousers and take himself in hand when light footsteps sounded outside the door.

"I miss them too," Collin said.

"Only them?" Tank asked.

Collin sighed. "Not only them. I miss Maureen and her cooking." He couldn't help smiling. "Oh, and Chip. I miss him too." There came that growl. "You know I wish I could be there, and I'll come for a visit as soon as I can. I promise. And you know there's always plenty of space for you here anytime you want. The men ask me when the cowboy from America is going to come back again. You made quite an impression. And just so you know, I want the cowboy from America—my *particular* cowboy from America—to come back anytime he wants." Bollocks, his voice actually broke, and that was the last thing he wanted. "I have to go," Collin said as a soft knock sounded on the door.

"Okay. I'll talk to you soon," Tank said, and Collin ended the call before opening the door.

"Yes, Tamsin," he said with a smile. "Are you about done for the day?" She was in her early thirties, pleasant, but incredibly quiet most of the time. At first he wondered if he and his father intimidated her, but he had come to understand that she believed it was part of her job to remain as inobtrusive as possible.

"Yes, sir. I also made a little supper. I brought the earl's in to him. Do you want me to come tomorrow?"

Collin nodded. "Would you like to work here as our housekeeper?" He had been working through a budget and had figured out a way to bring someone into the house to help him.

"Full-time?" she asked with the hint of a smile.

"Yes. You'd keep the house tidy and clean, as well as do some of the cooking. There are rooms for you in the house if you like as well. Though that's probably a little old-fashioned."

"I have a small house in the village, but I can come each morning." She smiled.

"Very good. I was hoping you'd agree, and thank you for seeing to my father."

"Of course," Tamsin said, making a little bow. "Thank you, sir."

"I'm Collin, not sir. And I should be thanking you." He motioned down the hall, and they headed toward the stairs. Collin let her go first, then followed her slowly down. "If you need someone to help with some of the heavier jobs, please let me know and we can make arrangements."

Tamsin paused at the base of the stairs. "So I'll be the head housekeeper?"

Collin grinned. "Yes. You can have any title you want." He stood at the bottom of the steps as Tamsin hurried off. He wished he could make himself that happy so easily.

After checking on his father, who had managed to eat most of his dinner, Collin took care of the dishes, then reheated the shepherd's pie Tamsin had left for him before going to the office to finish up for the day.

In the quiet room, with the last of the light coming through the windows, Collin swore he could almost see Tank riding across the lawn, chasing the wind. God, he really needed to get himself together.

Collin picked up the wedding invitation from the corner of the desk, wishing more than ever that he could take the time to go. George and Alan were planning their trip and had offered to take him with them. He ran through possibilities, but a thud pulled him out of his thoughts. He went through to the sitting room and found his father on the floor.

"I'm fine, boy. I was trying to get a book and misjudged the distance," his father snapped as Collin helped him up and back into the chair. Collin turned on the light near the chair, and his father settled back to read. Well, that settled that. He had to be here to look after his father, and going to Wyoming, no matter how much he wanted to, was out of the question. Collin returned to the office and figured he might as well find something to occupy his mind.

CHAPTER 17

MAUREEN AND Claude's wedding went off without a hitch, and they looked deliriously happy. Tank was so pleased for her and had been seated in the same row as Chip and Alan. That alone nearly brought him to tears. Maureen looked amazing as a bride, with flowers in her hair. Like any rancher worth her salt, she had arrived at the ceremony on the back of a horse, with Alan leading it. Then he'd walked his mother down the aisle and placed her in the care of her husband-to-be.

"What are you looking for?" Alan asked as Tank stood off to the side of the reception area behind Claude's impressive home. It was set up as a banquet for fifty and plenty of space left over.

"Nothing," he answered slowly.

Alan patted his shoulder once. "I know you were hoping Collin would be able to come, and he was trying to find a way. He even had someone lined up to come in and stay with his father while he was gone."

Tank nodded. "I know his father had another stroke and passed away two days ago." He swallowed hard. "Collin called and told me. He also said that in the past few weeks, the two of them had talked a lot more than they had in the past and that the earl seemed content."

"Yes. George and I offered to stay with him, but he told us the wedding was more important than the funeral. That he would be fine."

"I can't help wondering how he is going to do this all alone." He watched as people gathered around the immense deck and patio area, their happy voices intermingling. This was a celebration. Tank set his glass aside. "I'm sorry to be such a downer, but...."

Alan chuckled. "You're worried about him." He tilted his head slightly, and Claude approached. Tank forced a smile because he was not going to disrespect the groom on such a happy occasion. "Hi, Claude."

"Alan," he said with a smile. "Is there something you need?"

"No. But I think Tank needs to speak with you. I'm going to go get another drink and then dance with George." He headed off.

"Is there something you need from me?"

Claude shook his head as he watched his beautiful bride. "I have everything I need… and more. But I've been meaning to talk to you. I was going to wait until after the honeymoon, but Alan thought you might need to hear my thoughts."

Tank was intrigued.

"Maureen and I are going to manage our holdings together. She is coming to live with me, and the house and ranch will be run through my organization until Chip is ready to take over. He wants to become a vet, and Maureen and I want to support him." One thing Tank had to say about Claude, he was one of the most genuine and open people he had ever met. "The thing is that your piece of property, being right next to Maureen's holdings, will fit in well."

Tank narrowed his gaze. "You want to buy me out?"

Claude shook his head and smiled. "Not necessarily. I know that land has been in your family just like Maureen's has, as well as the core of my ranch. Generations of people put their blood, sweat, and tears into these places. But if you like, yes, I am willing to buy your spread. Or if you'd rather, I am more than willing to lease your land from you."

"Lease it?" Tank asked.

Claude nodded. "You have good rangeland and water access, and you connect to Maureen's property. Technically, she would be the one leasing your place. Think about it, and we can talk in the next few weeks." He gently patted Tank's back. "I do not want to do something that you aren't comfortable with, and if you wish to stay where you are, then there are no hard feelings and we'll be sure to be good neighbors. Give what I've said some thought."

Tank found himself nodding as Claude joined his bride and swept her out to dance. George and Alan joined them, as did other couples, and Tank wished he had Collin to dance with. Instead, he stood on the sidelines and watched the others.

THE PARTY went on well into the evening, but Tank said his goodbyes and went home. It was the wrong time to call Collin, so he sat up in the living room with a book, the dogs next to him on the sofa. Well, Sheba spent her time cuddled right next to him, and the two younger ones played on the floor most of the time before getting tired and joining their mother.

Tank should have been in bed long ago, and after reading the same paragraph three times, he set the book aside and texted Collin. When he got an answer right away, Tank phoned immediately.

"It's awfully early for you," Tank said.

"It's late for you," Collin retorted. "I was lying in bed, listening to this old house creak, and I figured I might as well get up. How was the wedding?"

"Very nice. Claude adores Maureen, and they both seemed to walk on air. They're the lesson that it's never too late for love."

"Why, Tank, you are a cowboy romantic," Collin told him, and Tank could feel the smile in his words. "I'm sorry I missed it. I've been making funeral arrangements, and it's proving trickier than I thought. Father had some wishes written down, and I have looked them over. He wanted a big funeral, but that isn't what's done any longer, so I decided to have a quieter ceremony on Thursday. I expect much of the village will turn up, or at least I hope they will." He sounded so tired. Tank lifted Sheba onto his lap and gently petted her. "You should get to bed, because you'll still have be up with the sun in the morning."

"And you should sleep so you can be ready for what comes next." Tank wished he was there with him so he could guide Collin back up those wide stairs and down that great hall to his bedroom.

Collin sighed. "Good night, Tank." He ended the call, and Tank figured it was time to go to bed. He had a ton of thinking to do.

CHAPTER 18

COLLIN WAS frayed to the edges of his nerves, but as far as he could tell, everything was set. He went over the last-minute details before climbing the stairs that were now his and going to his room. He dressed in black, as was traditional, before returning downstairs.

"Is there anything more that you need?" Tamsin asked.

"Thank you, no. You didn't need to come in today."

Tamsin nodded. "I know." She left the room. It was time to go, so Collin closed the front door behind him, got into the car, and drove to the village church. Walking into the building that had been there for centuries gave him a sense of solidity that otherwise seemed to have slipped out of his life. He sat down in front as others began to arrive.

Collin figured that he would use this time to think quietly and say his own goodbye to his father. It was funny—their final two weeks together were not what he would have expected, and Collin was glad they'd had them. The previous years had been full of tension and struggle. But those few weeks had been completely different. His father had even shared stories about his own childhood and his father, subjects he'd never talked about before.

"Do you mind if I sit here?"

Collin closed his eyes, knowing it had to be his imagination playing tricks on him. Slowly he lifted his gaze, and damn it all to hell, Tank stood at the end of the pew in a dark suit, a cowboy hat in hand.

"Is it really you?" Collin asked, not believing his eyes.

Tank sat down next to him, placing his hat on his lap. "You bet your ass." He bumped Collin's shoulder and then took his hand, squeezing his fingers.

"Why? How?" This was too damned much.

"I came because no one should have to say goodbye to their father without someone standing by them." He squeezed Collin's hand once again as people continued to fill the church. Collin lifted his gaze skyward and said a silent prayer, feeling for the first time that he was going to get through this day without shattering into a million tiny pieces.

"And I love you for it. You know that." Blast and hell, he was at a funeral, and this was so not the time to be professing his love, but he couldn't help it.

"I do." Tank said softly. Alan and the duke took their places on Collin's other side, and it seemed that neither of them had been aware of Tank's travel plans. Not that it mattered. This might have been a funeral, but in a way, Collin's real family had arrived in the nick of time, and he could finally release the breath he had been holding for days.

AT GEORGE'S recommendation, instead of having an after-funeral lunch, Collin bought out the pub in the village for the afternoon. He decided that rather than have a somber affair, he wanted to celebrate his father's life. Let folks tell their stories about his father and share their memories. There were some that Collin wanted to bury so deep they never resurfaced, but others he could talk about.

"Are you okay?" Tank asked when he approached Collin with a couple of pints of beer.

"I think so," Collin said, and drank the hoppy beverage before making another pass through the full room. He noticed as he passed how people's tone changed. They'd be laughing or telling some story about his father, but then as soon as he drew close, they would stiffen, their shoulders would shift, and then they'd clear their throats.

"You're the earl now," George told him as he and Alan stood near the end of the bar. "Before, you were the son, and you could have gotten away with being one of the guys. You can't do that any longer."

The room was full of people, but there was a ring of emptiness around the three of them—well, four when Tank joined them. Collin had never been so grateful for that light, warm touch of Tank's hand on his back. "The entire village will watch you and analyze every decision you make and everything they see."

Collin sighed. He knew it was true but had hoped to put it off as long as possible. It was amazing how he could be in a room full of people and still be alone. At the moment he wasn't alone, but the idea still hit him pretty hard. Maybe it had been just as hard for his father. "You have friends and people who like you for you," Tank said softly.

Alan nodded. "You do. And we don't care about titles and shit like that. We're cowboys. We can be an ass to everyone equally." He raised his glass, and Tank clinked it. George did the same, and Collin joined him, laughing softly, because how could he not.

Collin had paid the pub keeper enough for the party to go until five, but he skipped out early, just after George and Alan excused themselves. He had had more than enough at that point. Together they walked quietly back up toward the house, and Tank took his hand.

"How long can you stay?" Collin asked Tank as they walked.

"I'm not sure," Tank answered quietly. "But now is not the time to discuss it. I know you haven't slept well in days, I can see it in your eyes, and I know you're at the end of your energy." He squeezed Collin's hand. "Guys kept asking me how I knew the earl, and I listened to their stories."

"What did you say?"

"That I was a friend of the current earl," Tank whispered. "They would all smile and nod before returning to their story. It was kind of strange how they all behaved the same way."

Collin nodded. "I'm going to need to get used to it. I'm the earl, the guy who will make decisions they like and ones they don't. I'll be either the hero or the bad guy, sometimes in the same breath." He continued walking up the estate drive, then unlocked the main door and went inside.

His energy gave out almost as soon as Tank closed the door behind them. "Come on," Tank said softly before leading him upstairs.

"Where is your luggage?" Collin asked as he climbed.

"I put it in the office when I arrived. You had already left, but Tamsin let me in. It can stay there for the time being." Tank got him to his room and gently stripped off his coat and shirt. Once Collin kicked off his shoes, Tank got his pants off, and Collin nestled under the covers. Tank drew the curtains shut, darkening the room, before climbing under the covers next to him. Without thinking, Collin closed his eyes and did something he hadn't really done in days: slept.

"YOU DIDN'T want to talk about it yesterday," Collin said the following morning as he and Tank rode through the trees between the estate and the village. They had both gotten up early, and Collin figured a ride would help clear the cobwebs. "But how long are you staying?"

Tank pulled to a stop, their horses standing next to each other. Tank turned to look back, and Collin did the same, his gaze sweeping over the lawn leading to the house. "That depends on you," Tank said with a smile before slowly getting off his horse.

"It does?" Collin wasn't sure what Tank was getting at, but his heart did a little leap anyway as he dismounted and drew closer to Tank. He couldn't help tugging off Tank's hat and running his fingers through his soft black hair.

"Yeah. You know Maureen and Claude got married, and they plan to combine their cattle operations—well, in a way. I don't have all the details. But before they left on their trip, Claude talked to me, and then Maureen asked me to come over for breakfast. To make a long story short, they offered to buy my herd and lease my land for the next two years. There would still be details to work out, and I haven't given them an answer, but the long and short of it is that I can stay... if you want me."

Tank bit his lower lip. Collin's first instinct was to smile, but he didn't as a realization barreled into him. Tank was offering to come here to stay. He was willing to leave his life, his ranch, and everything he knew to be with Collin. His knees nearly buckled. "You're serious," he said.

"Yeah." Tank sounded so tentative.

"And you'll bring Sheba and the pups and stay here with me?" It was almost too good to be true.

"Like I said, if you want me." Those words sent a chill through Collin.

"Of course I want you," Collin said, throwing his arms around Tank's neck. "I've wanted you every day since you left." He kissed Tank hard before either of them could say anything more. Then those strong arms closed around his waist, and Collin groaned as he kissed Tank harder, ready to climb him right here and now. "You'll really stay?"

Tank nodded. "But there are a few conditions. The first is that you make an honest man out of me. And the second is that we need to discuss children." Tank stepped back and crossed his arms over his ample chest.

"Children?" Collin asked. It was something his father had brought up multiple times, but Collin honestly hadn't given it much thought.

"Yes. I want at least three. None of this only child stuff. I can teach them to ride and rope and how to be a cowboy, and you can teach them how to be ladies and gentlemen and the oldest to be a good earl once you and I go to the rangeland in the sky."

Collin nearly gasped. "You want children?"

Tank nodded. "But we have to do it so that our kids will be legitimate and can inherit. I want a little boy with your eyes and spirit running through that big house causing havoc, and a little girl with your red hair who can command a horse better than either of us could imagine. I want us to sit in that library together reading fantastic stories to them, and I want to take all of them back to America to show them where my people came from. I want to fill this place with dogs and animals and—"

"Life," Collin supplied, his hands shaking, damned near in tears. But he refused to let them fall. He was British, after all.

"Yes, and love, lots and lots of love." Tank caressed Collin's cheek. "I want to build a life here with you and fill this place with love." He motioned all around, and suddenly Collin had a vision of sorts. He and Tank at the stables, teaching their son how to ride his first pony, and Tank with a little girl on his lap, asleep in his arms, and Tank with his feet up, lying back as he hummed to her. For so long this place and his life here had been a struggle against his father, and maybe even more against the role he was expected to play. But with Tank, it felt different. Maybe between them, they could turn this old rambling place into a home.

Collin smiled and rested his head on Tank's shoulder. "I want all of that too." So badly he could almost taste it. "But are you sure?"

Tank drew him upward and kissed him hard, and this time he didn't let go until Collin whimpered. "Does that answer your question? I think it does," Tank said with a smile. "I think it answers everything." Then he kissed Collin once more.

EPILOGUE—A YEAR LATER

TANK STOOD at the edge of the lawn, looking back toward the house, his horse bouncing his head impatiently while Tank held the reins. He deeply inhaled the fresh air, smiling at the sight of his home. He never would have thought that twelve months could pass so quickly and with so much activity.

"What are you doing out here?" Collin asked as he rode up. "Chip, George, and Alan are going to be here in an hour." He grinned as he bounded off his horse and into Tank's arms.

"I know. I needed to clear my head a little." Tank hugged Collin, tucking him against his chest.

"There's nothing to worry about. You know that," Collin said. Chip had arrived a few days ago to stay with his brother and George for a couple of weeks.

"I know," Tank said. "It's just that I miss being back home sometimes. I grew up there." He didn't want to sound like a Debbie Downer. He didn't regret any of the decisions he'd made the last year.

"And we can go back to visit," Collin said.

"I know. But it doesn't make any sense to keep the house and land when I'm only there a few weeks a year." He had been thinking a lot lately. Maureen still had a year to go on their lease agreement, but he was thinking that maybe he should sell. It would be to people he thought of as family, and Tank knew they would treat the land well. "This is my home now."

Collin sniffed slightly. "Do you know how long I've waited to hear that?"

"I know, and it's taken me longer than I expected to feel it, but it's a fact. This land and the people on it are home." It helped that Collin let Tank oversee the estate's livestock operations. It gave him something of his own. His first task had been managing the sale of Collin's father's string of polo ponies. Many of the animals had indeed been purchased by team members, while others had been incorporated into strings throughout the country. Tank had to admit that Collin's father had an eye for good horses, and the proceeds of the sale had been nearly enough to pay the death duties on the estate. Not only that, but the reduction in expenses had pushed the estate into a more profitable status, which gave Collin room to maneuver financially. "It's just hard to let go."

"I understand, and you don't need to make this decision now. You still have time," Collin said.

"I know I do. But I think in my heart I know what I want. I just have to bring that last part of myself along." And he figured the easiest way to do that was to make a decision and then move forward. "I can't have one leg in the past and the other in our future. So with that in mind, there isn't much of a choice to make." Tank glanced around, wishing they were out of sight of the house. He was tempted to take Collin into the woods and get him to scream his passion to the trees, but they didn't have time for that. "Come on." He pushed those thoughts from his head, because riding a horse with a boner was always a bad idea.

They started back toward the stables, where they saw to their mounts before walking over the lawn to the house. They cleaned up, and Tank got out the munchies Tamsin had prepared and set them up in the library as the bell rang. Collin got the door with Tank behind him, and the five men shared hugs before Collin showed Chip around and Tank took George and Alan into the library to talk business. They had worked together to combine the strengths of their two estates. Both of their stables were now full with mostly paying boarders. George specialized in racing, while Tank worked with horses that needed to be rehabilitated like Barney, who they had brought over. He still wasn't much for being ridden, but he'd calmed down a lot, and his stud shares were in huge demand. The three of them talked strategy and training until Collin and Chip joined them with Sheba, Liza, and Danny right behind, fanning out to get attention.

"The house is looking great," Chip said. "You really made the day room beautiful, and the dining room is amazing. Was all that trim and the paintings there?"

"Yeah. The trim was under old ceiling repairs that we removed, and the original frescos were under the old wallpaper, just waiting to be discovered and conserved." Collin sat next to Tank. "We're working on the library. The woodwork in here is being cleaned, with just that final section to go. We have a librarian who is helping us put the books back in order."

Chip made his way around the room, looking at each section of shelving.

"Is that the secret door?" Chip asked.

"Yes. We've had people in to try to open it, but with no key, the only choice is to dismantle the shelving, and we don't want to do that. So we keep looking."

Chip continued his circuit of the library.

"How soon before you're ready to add the house to the tour?"

"How about Christmas?" Collin answered. "You run those special openings in December, and we thought we'd open during that period and then join with your schedule starting in the spring."

"Do you have a theme for the holiday?" George asked, and he and Collin batted around various ideas while Chip continued looking over the room itself. Tank joined him as he stared into the corner.

"What's wrong?"

Chip shrugged. "I don't know. This looks off somehow." He ran his fingers over the decorative moldings that had yet to be cleaned. Then he looked toward the other corner.

"I get it. The corner should be the same, but it's different." Tank pressed on the molding, and it slid downward. He pressed harder, and a four-inch piece slid farther down, revealing a space that held some papers. Tank gently lifted them out and found a key at the bottom. He turned and showed the key to Collin before handing him the pages.

"What is this?" Collin asked, going to the library table.

"It's a letter... from the fifth earl," George said. "This has been in there for more than a century and a half. Get some gloves, and don't touch the papers again until you do." Tank hurried to the kitchen and retuned with a pair of white cotton gloves. He handed them to Collin, who carefully spread out the pages.

"It's almost pristine, except for the yellowing," Collin said.

> *To my descendant who finds this:*
> *My son will inherit the estate, and there is nothing*
> *I can do about it. The entail and tradition are too strong*
> *for me to stop it. But he spends more time in the taverns*
> *and gambling dens than is good for him. So as part of*

repairing the library, I had this hiding space built, as
well as one behind the case across the room. If you look
closely, you'll find the keyhole. Over the last year I have
removed a number of important and historical items
from the house and placed them behind the bookcase
because the sixth earl is certain to sell anything he is
able to in order to support his vices.

Collin raised his gaze. "I'll be damned. There are stories of the fifth earl selling a number of items." He became breathless. "At least that's what we always thought. My grandfather was a stickler about trying to preserve what we had and did his best to add to the family collection. I don't think my father cared either way."

"What is supposed to have been sold?" George asked, but Collin was already at the case.

Collin placed the key in the hole and smiled back at Tank when it turned. He pulled carefully, and the case slid back slightly before swinging open. Chip thankfully kept the dogs from racing forward.

"Oh my God," George gasped. "Good Lord."

Tank stood behind Collin and peered inside. "Can you tell me what I'm looking at?"

"It seems that Collin's great-great grandfather built this almost two hundred years ago at the beginning of the Victorian period and...." George seemed to lose his voice. "Let me see. That right there is Elizabeth the First, that is Charles the Second, and that one right there is Queen Mary, if I'm not mistaken. Those look like Italian renaissance, and that...." George's voice stopped. "I'm willing to guess that all of these are works that the world has classified as lost."

Tank looked closer. The room was about ten feet long all told, and about two feet deep. The paintings hung on the back wall, and Tank supposed it was lucky that none of them had fallen down or out of their frames. They were covered in dust, but the light from the library was enough to make them visible. "What's all that?"

"I don't know," Collin said. "I'm going to need to call the conservator and ask him to come over and remove all the items. I don't want to touch them as they are."

"I'll get a torch." Tank went to the office and returned with a small flashlight that he shone back into the darkness. Sculptures stood on stone pedestals to one side, and on the other side, a built-in shelf was covered with smaller items.

Tank backed out to give each of the others a chance to look before they all exited and Collin closed the door, pushing it back into place. He didn't lock it this time before sitting back down. "I can't believe it. Everything is there. My grandfather used to lament the loss of all those things, and damn, he had no idea they were right behind there his entire life."

"What are we going to do with them?" Tank asked.

Collin smiled. "We're going to conserve them, then hang them and put them on public display." He sat next to Tank and munched on a chip, then turned to Tank. "Finding all that has been the second-best thing to happen today."

"Second best?" George asked as the dogs joined them on the sofa, tails wagging as they found their spots.

"Yeah. Tank has said he's going to sell his ranch to Maureen and make his permanent home here with me." Collin leaned over to Tank, gazing into his cowboy's deep eyes. "That is worth more than all the found treasures in the world."

Tank couldn't help thinking that being speechless was sometimes the best thing ever.

Keep reading for an excerpt from
Buck Me
by Andrew Grey.

CHAPTER 1

ANOTHER DAY on the ranch for Emmett Beauregard McElroy, and yeah, that was a mouthful if he ever heard one. Everyone called him Emmett or Em, thank God. When he was a baby, his mama had thought they could call him EBM or some damned thing, but his father thought it sounded like an out-of-control bowel condition and nixed it. There was precedent for using initials. His older brother, Robert Edward, had been RE, and that worked, but Emmett preferred that people use his name, especially the hands on his family ranch.

The horses, of course, didn't give a damn. Though if the horse he was working with could actually talk like Mr. Ed, he might have an easier time with the beast.

"Okay, hold still," Emmett said in as soft a voice as he could muster with Virginia. She was a champion cutting horse, the pride of the McElroy stables and the most cantankerous mare Emmett had ever met. And that was saying something. "Now just lift your foot so I can get the stone out for you."

Emmett did all the right things. He never made quick movements and never raised his voice. He was the epitome of calm as he got to the stone and pulled it out from where her hoof met the shoe. The farrier was scheduled to be out in a day or so. All he wanted to do was make her more comfortable and ensure that there wasn't any damage to the tender portion of the hoof. "There you go. That should be better." He lowered her leg and felt up it for any heat. There was none, thank God. His father would have a screaming fit if anything happened to her. "Do you want me to brush you?" He refused to show the hesitation he felt crawling under his skin.

She stomped her front hooves, and Emmett took a step back to let her get out any orneriness, then bent to get the brush from where it had fallen onto the concrete floor. A sharp pinch grabbed his ass, and he jumped about two feet straight up.

"Dammit!" He straightened fast, jumping forward as Virginia neighed, or made a sound as close to a laugh as the she-devil horse could muster. "Fine. One of the guys can brush you, ya old pain in the butt." In more ways than one.

He took her by the halter, unfastened her from the leads, and led her through the barn to her stall, then closed the damned door with more force than necessary. After putting the supplies away, he stomped out of the stable and across the yard, rubbing his right buttcheek.

"Did she bite you?" Holace asked. The bastard had the gall to actually laugh.

"Yes." Emmett turned with a hard glare.

Holace didn't even try to hide his mirth. "At least you have a matched set. Didn't Reggie get your other cheek a few days ago?"

He had, dammit. The last time he'd checked, his left buttcheek had been black and blue. Now the other was going to be the same. "Nice to know you have such a fascination with my asscheeks. Maybe you'd like to come over here and take a look?" Emmett winked, and Holace stumbled a second. His whole family and the dozen or so hands on the ranch knew he was gay. After all, there had been enough screaming, name calling, and stomping from his dad that all of central Montana knew exactly what was going on. Tears and worry from his mama, who could be just as dramatic in her own way. Needless to say, the fact that Emmett preferred bulls to heifers wasn't a secret.

"I don't want to be hearing about that gay stuff," Holace called back.

Emmett couldn't resist. "Then don't go taking an interest in my ass. I might take it as an invitation." He winked, and Holace stilled for a second before throwing his head back with a hearty laugh.

Emmett turned and walked away, but he resisted rubbing his butt again until he was out of sight. Damn, that hurt. For the past two days, he had sat to one side because of the soreness. Now that was shot to hell. But how was he going to explain to his mama that he needed to stand during dinner because a damn horse tried to bite a piece of his butt… again? He needed to get his mind on the tasks at hand, rather than worrying about stuff he couldn't change. This was his job, and like it or not, he needed to keep his nerves under control and his head in the game.

As soon as he stepped into the sprawling ranch house where he'd grown up, the scent of roasting chicken and a touch of vinegar reached his nose. He knew that meant coleslaw and probably mashed potatoes to go with the chicken. Emmett's stomach growled, and for a few seconds he forgot about his aching buttcheeks.

"That smells amazing, Martha," he said, taking off his boots before going to the large kitchen at the back of the house. Their cook and housekeeper took good care of him.

"I know it's your favorite," she said with a smile as she poured shredded cabbage into a large bowl. "I know what this family likes."

Emmett kissed her cheek and stole a taste of the salad. She scolded him, and he scooted out of the kitchen.

"Where's Mama?" Emmett asked.

"I think she's in her work room trying not to swear at her sewing machine," Martha said softly. Everyone knew his mother wouldn't say *shit* if she had a mouth full of it. Still, he smiled and thanked her before going down the hall and pausing outside the closed door. Muttering drifted through the door, and he knocked before opening it.

"What has you so riled up?" Emmett asked.

She huffed and then set aside the dress she was working on, turning with a smile. "You weren't supposed to hear that. Why do you think I had the door closed?" Her eyes were hard, even if the rest of her expression was completely composed. Giselle Eugenia Lafont McElroy had been raised as a Southern debutant, complete with cotillion lessons, afternoon tea, lessons in deportment, and even training in the arts, including painting and music. She could converse on any topic and entertain a room full of strangers as though they were old friends. She also believed that any unseemly behavior that might occur alone and behind closed doors simply didn't count—especially if it was hers. "Did you finish up with the horses? Dustin asked if you'd been in as he breezed through for lunch."

"Of course he did," Emmett said. He was surprised his father hadn't stopped in the barn to check up on him. Maybe he had and just hadn't made his presence known. His dad loved being stealthy. When Emmett was a kid, he used to think he was so clever, but every night at dinner, all the things he'd thought he'd gotten away with were discussed in front of everyone. That might have been okay if his older brother, RE, and his sister, Suzanne, had gotten the same treatment. They didn't. RE was always the golden child, the oldest and apple of his father's eye, and Suzanne, well, she was the only daughter. Emmett just seemed to exist in RE's shadow, until he was gone. And now Emmett was expected to fill his shoes. "The day he doesn't check up on me like I'm an errant teenager who doesn't know shit around here is the day he dies." It got so that Emmett could eat a full meal in five minutes and be gone from the table faster. That meant Dad had less time to enumerate his seemingly ever-growing list of faults. Emmett turned to leave his mother alone. His patience was wearing thin just talking about his father, and he didn't want to take it out on her.

"Watch your language," his mother scolded.

Emmett snickered. "I heard worse coming out of you through the door." It wasn't often that he got one up on his mama. In their family, his father, Dustin, wore the pants, but there was no doubt that his mama wore the genteel, pointed-toed shoes that could kick those pants right in the ass. "Where is Dad, anyway?"

"He was out with the men checking on the herd. He got some reports that one of the watering holes was getting a little low, so he went to check to see if some of the herd needed to be driven to lower ground." She turned back to the sewing machine. "Go and get yourself cleaned up and ready for dinner. I'm going to fight with the gather on this dress for a few more minutes." He turned. "And close the door." Apparently, the gather was going to require more words she didn't want to actually put out into the universe.

Emmett went to his room and closed the door. The one thing he had been able to convince his father to do for him had been to combine two of the smaller back bedrooms into one with its own bathroom. The work had been completed only a few months ago, and it had only happened because Suzanne would be moving out soon for her first year of medical school. RE... well, he was gone, and the loss of his older brother still hurt.

He winced as he gingerly sat on the edge of his bed, looking at the picture of himself and his brother, taken at Emmett's high school graduation. Emmett was gawky in his dark blue cap and gown, firmly in his brother's shadow. RE stood next to him, tall, broad, with bright eyes and a huge smile. The thing was that Emmett probably should have hated his perfect older brother. He'd been Dad's favorite and did no wrong, but RE had always made time for Emmett, encouraged him like his father never did, and even tried to teach him how to ride on numerous occasions. Not that it ever worked. He was nervous around horses and consequently they hated him, and he had the broken leg, two broken arms, and ending-up-on-his-ass-in-the-dirt more times than he could count to prove it. Maybe it was one of those circular logic sorts of things, his nerves making the horses hate him and then the horses making him nervous. But RE never gave up, and when he got hurt, it had been RE who took him to the hospital and sat with him while the doctor set his latest broken bone or stitched closed the cuts. It had been RE who looked out for him and stood up for him when he'd sneak off to the hayloft to read rather than shovel horse shit. It had been RE that he'd first told that he was gay, and his brother had not only hugged him and said it would be okay, but he kept his secret as far as Emmett knew—he'd said that was the sort of thing a man had to be the one to decide when he wanted folks to know. "Damn, RE, if you could see what Dad has me doing now, you'd probably crap yourself laughing." Managing the horses on the Rolling D had been RE's job. But then his brother died when a semi plowed into his truck, and now it fell to Emmett. The shock of RE's death had nearly killed his parents, and in some ways they had yet to recover. Emmett knew he was a poor substitute for his brother, but he always did his best… and had the sore ass to prove it.

He stripped out of his clothes and hit the shower, checking his backside in the mirror. Sure enough, he was indeed going to have another livid bruise. Not that it mattered, because no one was going to see his bare ass except him. Emmett washed quickly and dressed in a clean pair of jeans and a red polo shirt Suzanne had given him for Christmas last year. His mother insisted that they look nice for dinner, and not even his father dared contradict her. Jeans were only recently allowed. When he was a child, it had been dress pants and a church-worthy shirt for dinner every night. Talk about torture.

"Do you need any help?" Emmett asked Martha as he passed through the kitchen.

"No. I have everything under control. Your dad came in ten minutes ago, and he's in the living room with your mama." They always shared a glass of wine or a cocktail before dinner. It seemed out of place on the ranch, but it was one of Mama's rituals, and Dad liked to keep her happy.

"Then you're sure there isn't something I can do?" He snatched a carrot off the counter, munching on it and getting out of her way as she pulled open the oven door. Avoiding his dad was becoming his sport of choice.

"Go on in. Your dad seemed in a good mood," Martha said and shooed him out of the kitchen. Not that he wanted to piss her off. Martha took care of the entire family, but she always especially looked out for him. When he was little, she always had a cookie ready when things between him and his dad went to crap. To his father, Emmett should be a cowboy, like everyone else in the family, but Emmett had other interests—like books and even sketching and art—that his father didn't see as cowboy-like. Not that Emmett was particularly talented, but those things didn't involve horses and tying his belly in knots. The nights he ran from the table under his dad's sometimes withering criticism, she'd sneak a sandwich and a chocolate chip cookie to his room so he didn't go hungry.

"Good to know," he said softly and went into the living room, where he poured himself a glass of the wine his folks were drinking. His mother knew all about wine and made sure that there were always good bottles in the cellar. Emmett knew what he liked, though he preferred beer or a mixed drink.

"I went looking for you," his dad said as soon as Emmett set the bottle back on the tray. "But you were busy."

"Of course I was," Emmett retorted. "I'm always busy."

"Sit down," his mother said.

"I'm fine." Emmett wasn't going to explain in front of his dad that he'd gotten his ass bitten… again. Still, he turned to him. "Was everything up to your illustrious standards?" He drank half the glass of wine in a few gulps.

"Don't be a smartass," his father snapped.

"Then stop acting like I'm still a kid to be scolded." He'd managed the cutting horse portion of the family business for the five years since RE's accident, stepping into his older brother's shoes because his father expected it. Emmett had hoped to leave the ranch to make his own way in the world, become a high-powered businessman or a lawyer, or maybe an astronaut. Unlike most kids, his dreams didn't involve horses. Nonetheless, most of the time he'd even learned to manage his nerves around them.

Dad ran the entire family business but concentrated on the cattle portion. It was much larger and provided the bulk of the business income. All his life, Emmett felt as though he tried to live up to his father's expectations and fell short. With RE gone, it seemed as though he fell shorter and farther from the mark of what his dad wanted, probably because he just wasn't his brother. No matter what he did, things weren't right, even when Emmett knew he was doing exactly what his father ·would in the same circumstances.

The back door closed, and Suzanne called to announce that she was home. Emmett glared into his father's intense blue eyes and then turned to his mother, then back to his dad. "I don't know what time you started this morning, but you were snoring loud enough to wake the dead when I got up and started before you." He finished his wine and set the glass down before meeting Suzanne with a hug. "Hey, sissy."

She returned it. "Going a round with Dad, Em?" she whispered as she gave his backside a pat—her older-sister way of letting him know that she knew what happened. He stifled a hiss and stepped away from her.

"Here, honey, have a glass of wine," his father said, suddenly all smiles. "How was the visit?"

"Perfect. I have everything all set, classes all registered, and I found out the books I'm going to need. They're being shipped here so I can work through them in the next two weeks. The first year of med school is a killer, and I'm going to be ready." She was always top of her class in everything. Determined and driven, she and Emmett had been close growing up, but their lives seemed on different paths now. "How are the horses, Em?" Dang, she could be wicked when she wanted to be. She winked to say she was only teasing.

"Good. Virginia is as ornery as ever," he told her. "Holace is doing some amazing work with the others, and we're going to have a wonderful crop of cutting horses to sell on the open market in a few months." Each of their horses, with their bloodlines and training, sold for tens of thousands of dollars.

"I saw him working with the yearlings," his dad said. "He looked good. Maybe next week I'll come by and do an evaluation." He finished his wine and leaned back in his seat before burping softly.

"No need. They aren't ready yet. It will be a few months." Emmett might not have a rapport with the horses, but he knew well enough that none were ready. Still, his father would step in, look things over, and come to the same conclusion that he did, only with a side of grief and disruption.

"Dustin, let Emmett do his job," his mother said softly, even as his dad stared a hole in him.

Emmett returned his father's dead-reckoning stare. He used to think his father could see into his soul with that look on his weathered, suntanned face. Dustin McElroy was every inch a cowboy, pure and simple—everything Emmett knew he would never be—and sometimes the disappointment in his father's eyes was more than he could stand. "It's fine. Dad can come by any time he wants." Emmett tried to keep the hurt and frustration out of his voice.

Fortunately, Martha came in to say that dinner was ready. That ended the staring contest, but nothing was going to change between them. Maybe they were both too stubborn for their own good.

Martha had dinner on the table, and the five of them took their places. It had taken Mama a long while before she could convince Martha to eat dinner with them. "Where's Marianne?" Suzanne asked as their father started passing the food around the table.

"She's having dinner with some friends," Martha answered with a smile. Marianne was Martha's only child and the apple of her eye. She also had a tongue as sharp as a knife and said what was on her mind. There had been many times when she'd left Emmett completely gobsmacked, and his little gay cowboy heart loved her for it.

Even though Mama knew Emmett was gay—he had the tearstained handkerchief to prove it—she still held out hope that he and Marianne would get together. She pushed them on each other at every opportunity. Even if he weren't gay, Marianne was almost as much a sister to him as Suzanne was, and the idea of getting together with her felt wrong on every level.

"When does she return to school?" Emmett asked. Marianne was entering her senior year at the University of Montana.

"A couple months." Martha smiled and yet seemed like she might cry at the same time. "Just the rest of the summer, and then my baby will be completely out on her own."

Mama took Martha's hand and looked at Suzanne. "I know exactly what you mean."

"If you got your head screwed on straight, you could marry that girl, make both your mama and her mama happy, settle down, and maybe start filling this house with little McElroys to carry on the family name," his father growled, and then put his hand to his chest. He patted it gently and set down his fork. He drank some water and sat still.

"Dustin?" his mother asked.

"Just a little indigestion. Been belching all day." He performed a demonstration and picked up his fork.

Mama rolled her eyes. "Dustin, you may be doing it, but you don't need to talk about it at the table," she scolded gently and continued watching him until he began eating again.

Emmett shook his head. He had heard that little aria about him and Marianne more times than he could count, and every time he tried to argue, his mother got upset and his father got angry. It was a familiar tune, and every time he came out a loser, so he lowered his gaze and returned to his dinner, eating quickly so he could escape and just get away.

"Sorry, Em," Suzanne whispered to him and continued eating. He noticed her sympathy, but also that she didn't stand up for him either. Emmett had long ago learned that his sister loved being Daddy's little girl, and she wasn't about to do anything to jeopardize his view of her.

He shrugged. "You know, Mama, maybe it's time I do what Suzanne and Marianne did. I've been thinking of taking the college entrance tests and looking into classes, probably business. I was always good at math and things like that." After high school he had wanted to go away to college himself, but RE passed away, so he'd put that on hold to help his family. Now he really hoped he could go.

The look that passed between his parents was unmistakable. Disappointment… again. Maybe he should have those words tattooed on each of his bruised buttcheeks.

Since RE's death, he had been expected to fill his impossibly big shoes, and that meant being the heir apparent, learning the ranch, taking his brother's position, and eventually assuming control of the ranch from his father. Whether he wanted to or not was as unrelated as deep-sea fishing and the Montana Rockies. He took the last bite of his dinner and pushed back his chair. "Thank you, Martha. That was delicious as always." He gave her a smile and stood, thankful to be upright and off his aching backside. "I have some things I need to check in the stables."

His mama gave him one of her patented unhappy looks with her eyes hard and her mouth set.

"The boy has things to do." His father reached for his water with his right hand and slopped it all down his front before dropping the glass to the floor, where it shattered. He placed his hands on his chest, gasping for air as he leaned back in the chair and began to slump under the table. Suzanne jumped up and helped catch him.

"Call an ambulance, Mama," Suzanne said with authority. "Now!" she added when Giselle didn't move. Emmett pulled out his phone, made the call, and handed the phone to his mother while he helped Suzanne get his father out of the chair.

Emmett lifted his dad—he had no idea how—and carried him to the sofa, where Suzanne took over his care. He stepped back, with Mama looking fearfully at his father, who was still clutching his chest. He was as white as a sheet. Mama held the phone to her ear as she knelt next to the sofa and held his father's hand.

After the longest fifteen minutes in history, sirens sounded and drew closer, and then an ambulance pulled into the yard. "I'll go with him," Mama said.

"Okay," Suzanne agreed as the EMTs raced inside. Only then did Mama end the call and hand Emmett back his phone. "Emmett and I will follow you."

His father grabbed Emmett's hand and tugged him close, pain in the blue eyes that usually only displayed stubborn strength. "Son...." He leaned closer, his voice weak and soft, deep lines etched around his eyes and mouth.

"Yeah, Dad," Emmett said, swallowing hard. "Don't try to talk. Save your strength."

He squeezed Emmett's hand and winced. "Stay here. Someone has to look over the horses and cattle." His father let go, and Emmett backed away, a sense of renewed rejection washing over him, but he pushed it away. If his father wanted him to look after the ranch, then he would do his best to make his father proud.

Scan the QR Code below to order.

ANDREW GREY is the author of more than two hundred works of Contemporary Gay Romantic fiction. After twenty-seven years in corporate America, he has now settled down in Central Pennsylvania with his husband of more than twenty-five years, Dominic, and his laptop. An interesting ménage. Andrew grew up in western Michigan with a father who loved to tell stories and a mother who loved to read them. Since then he has lived throughout the country and traveled throughout the world. He is a recipient of the RWA Centennial Award, has a master's degree from the University of Wisconsin–Milwaukee, and now writes full-time. Andrew's hobbies include collecting antiques, gardening, and leaving his dirty dishes anywhere but in the sink (particularly when writing). He considers himself blessed with an accepting family, fantastic friends, and the world's most supportive and loving partner. Andrew currently lives in beautiful, historic Carlisle, Pennsylvania.

Email: andrewgrey@comcast.net
Website:www.andrewgreybooks.com

How can they be together when
they live in different worlds?

The Duke's Cowboy

COWBOY NOBILITY ♥ BOOK ONE

ANDREW GREY

Cowboy Nobility: Book One

George Lester, the Duke of Northumberland, flees familial expectations in Britain for the promise of freedom of San Francisco, looking for the chance to be himself. But before he even gets close, a blizzard forces him off the road, and he finds himself freezing half to death in a small town with no motel... with a litter of puppies to look after.

Luckily for George, he also finds Alan.

As the heir to his family's ranch, Alan Justice knows the burden of being the oldest son. He doesn't have time to show George, the stranger his brother dragged home, what it takes to be a cowboy. But that very night, George surprises him by helping a mare in distress through a difficult birth. Maybe the duke is made of sterner stuff than Alan thought.

George and Alan keep surprising each other, and every day they grow a little closer. But when George's responsibilities call him home, Alan finds he's the one who has something to prove—that he can handle what it means to be the duke's cowboy.

Scan the QR Code below to order.

DEDICATED
TO YOU

ANDREW GREY

Dillon Fitzgerald is a famous singer. He's also exhausted. Too many shows in a too busy schedule have left too little time for him to write or relax. He feels like the music is being strangled out of him. Some time is just what the doctor ordered, so when his friend offers him a week on a cruise, Dillon gets right on board. All he has to do is grow a little beard and hope no one recognizes him.

Financial advisor Tio Smythe-Barrett has been friends with Dillon forever. When the latest in a long string of girlfriends turns out to be a cheater, Tio offers her spot on what would have been a romantic vacation to Dillon instead. After all, why wouldn't he want to spend a week with his best friend?

As Tio and Dillon share close quarters, the boundaries in their friendship shift like the ocean currents. Spending time with Tio has Dillon's creative muse singing, and he can no longer deny that his feelings for Tio go beyond friendship. His heart soars when Tio responds to his flirting—but is he willing to risk what they have for the chance at true love?

Scan the QR Code below to order.

THROUGH the FLAMES
ANDREW GREY

Carlisle
Fire

1

Carlisle Fire: Book One

Kyle Wilson hasn't had it easy. His insecurities and nasty home life made him lash out as a kid, and when he finally came out as gay, his family disowned him. Then, just when he's pulled his life together and gotten his construction company running, he's caught in a fire and forced to take costly time off.

When firefighter Hayden Walters rescues a man from a burning building, he's just doing his job. He doesn't expect it to turn his life upside-down, but the man is none other than Hayden's high school bully.

He definitely doesn't expect Kyle to come to the station to thank him in person.

With awkward apologies out of the way, Kyle and Hayden realize they have a lot in common. And when it turns out someone set the fire at Kyle's construction site to target him, they find they can solve each other's problems too: Hayden needs a place to stay while his apartment is renovated, and Kyle doesn't want to be alone in case the firebug strikes again. Things between the two of them quickly heat up—but so does the arsonist's agenda. Can they track down the would-be killer before it's too late?

Scan the QR Code below to order.

ONLY
THE
BRIGHTEST
STARS

ANDREW
GREY

The problem with being an actor on top of the world is that you have a long way to fall.

Logan Steele is miserable. Hollywood life is dragging him down. Drugs, men, and booze are all too easy. Pulling himself out of his self-destructive spiral, not so much.

Brit Stimple does whatever he can to pay the bills. Right now that means editing porn. But Brit knows he has the talent to make it big, and he gets his break one night when Logan sees him perform on stage.

When Logan arranges for an opportunity for Brit to prove his talent, Brit's whole life turns around. Brit's talent shines brightly for all to see, and he brings joy and love to Logan's life and stability to his out-of-control lifestyle. Unfortunately, not everyone is happy for Logan, and as Brit's star rises, Logan's demons marshal forces to try to tear the new lovers apart.

Scan the QR Code below to order.

First impressions are never what they seem.

LOST
AND
FOUND

ANDREW GREY

Rafe Carrera hasn't seen his Uncle Mack since he was a kid, so when he inherits his ranch, it throws him like a bucking horse. He's been on his own for a long time. Now suddenly everyone wants to be his friend... or at least get friendly enough to have a chance in buying the ranch.

Russell Banion's family may own a mega-ranch in Telluride, but Russell made his own way developing software. He misses his friend Mack, and purchasing the ranch will help him preserve Mack's legacy—and protect his own interests. It's a win-win. Besides, spending time with Rafe, trying to soften him up, isn't exactly a hardship. Soon Russell realizes he'll be more upset if Rafe does decide to leave.

But Rafe isn't sure he wants to sell. To others in the valley, his land is worth more than just dollars and cents, and they'll do anything to get it. With Russell's support, Rafe will have to decide if some things—like real friendship, neighborliness, and even love—mean more than money.

Scan the QR Code below to order.